# Moose's Regret

Haven MC
Book One

by Carson Mackenzie

CM Books, LLC

Published by CM Books, LLC
Previously published under the title – Snatched
Copyright © July 2016 Carson Mackenzie
Cover Design by Carson Mackenzie
ISBN# 978-1-952184-20-8

CM Books, LLC

# Synopsis

Linc Harris found a home at Haven MC, one that came with men whom he was honored to call his brothers. The club has suffered from some internal issues, and it is time to put them to rest and set Haven on a new path. But in doing so, Moose's past, one he thought he had neatly tucked away, is brought front and center. It isn't one he really ever wanted to let go; it was just one he'd hoped to settle when he was ready.

Kathryn Stevens has reached her dream of becoming a doctor, and she did it even while putting her heart back together. She refuses to allow anyone in who could open those wounds again, so when she is targeted to be used as a pawn, she gets the opportunity to test her resolve. But she is the first to admit, the man who caused her to even implement the resolve—is the only one she would trust to save her.

Join the men of Haven MC as they prove that not only should you never judge a book by its cover, you shouldn't judge men for the sole fact they ride Harleys and wear leather.

CM Books, LLC

CM Books, LLC

# Table of Contents

CM Books, LLC

CM Books, LLC

# Prologue

## Moose

William Borelli was one of the few men I had encountered who matched me in size and height. I stood in the office of the Haven MC president and waited to see if I was going to be allowed in the club.

"Prospecting is a way for clubs to learn about a man and what he is made of. It's a thankless job within a club because you are expected to do everything asked of you without question. There is no set time to be patched in as a full member; it all depends on performance—how the others accept you—loyalty to the club and its leadership. So, it is up to the Prospect on how fast or slow that patching in timeframe goes." Wild Bill frowned but never broke eye contact with me. "Haven is dealing with a few problems, ones that are currently being looked at to get to the bottom of the issue. It is going to be a slow process, but this club has been around awhile, it will weather this too," the Prez said and walked around his desk and sat down, pointing to the

9

chair across from him. I took a seat and leaned forward and placed my elbows on my knees.

"Alright," I said as I watched the Prez's face for signs of where this might be going. My knowledge of MCs was minimal, to say the least, but I couldn't imagine the president of an MC handling a prospective member in his office without any of the other leaders present.

"You come highly recommended, Linc." I frowned at his words, and Wild Bill continued. "Hawk, Keg, Pinch, Crank, and Tram are Prospects already. Having you come on board would be a great addition," he finished.

"What do you mean I come highly recommended? I feel like this is more than a wanna-be part of my club talk. The word I've heard around town since I rode in, is that whatever I did, I needed to stay clear of Haven's members. Met Hawk at that bar about a week ago. We talked, and he is the one who said Haven was recruiting members. Gotta say, though, I'm questioning what kinda members?" I watched Wild Bill's eyes change, his pupils lighten, and a small twitch to his lips as if he was fighting to keep a smile off his face, all as he stared back at me. He leaned back in his chair, crossed his arms over his chest, and minutes ticked by as I waited for him to respond.

Wild Bill uncrossed his arms, leaned forward, and placed his elbows on the desk before he spoke, "Let me give you some information and then when I am done, you can decide if Haven fits you. Fair enough?"

"Yes," was the only reply I gave.

CM Books, LLC

"I'm sure you've been told that Haven has been around for a while. It was started by my grandfather during a time when MCs were all considered to be run by men who were no better than the average outlaw, all because they had different views on how they wanted to live, versus what the majority of people thought was acceptable. Not going to get into the 'my opinion is right, and your opinion is wrong' debate that nowadays seems to fit with anything anyone does or says in society.

"My dad took over for his father as president when my grandfather was diagnosed with lung cancer. William Sr. was a hard man and ran Haven with a firm hand, my dad, not so much. Drugs, guns, you name it was and is still going on in Haven. I took over when my dad was killed due to the illegal activity the club was in. I'm not going to go into detail on everything that is going on right now, but I will do a quick recap." I nodded, and Wild Bill continued. "There are members of this club who had an issue when I stepped in for my dad. I will admit the illegal activity grew more after my own wife and ol' lady became sick right after I had stepped in. Not using it as an excuse, but I did check out for a while, Sami was young, and Reed was a teenager, my plate was full. I pulled myself together, but... It is what it is. I can see in your eyes that you are trying to figure out exactly why we are having this talk, when what you thought was just an informal meeting to see about prospecting for us. If you decide to join, you will be a Prospect like I said before. We are an MC in all aspects; some of us are just a little more."

"How much more?" I asked when he finished.

"That can be discussed if you decide to stay." Wild Bill sat up in his chair.

"Gonna admit not well versed on MCs, other than what I've read and stuff, but I can't imagine you sharing everything with a Prospect even if I do this," I said and cocked my brow and waited.

"You are right to a point, but I was talking about the *more* part," Wild Bill replied.

If I said I wasn't interested, it would be a lie. I liked the guys I'd met so far from Haven.

"What would keep me from saying yes, and you tell me everything, then I walk away?" I asked and watched the smile form on Wild Bill's face.

"Nothing. Just as it would be nothing to me if you came up missing," Wild Bill and never lost the smile on his face when he made the statement.

I sat quietly and stared at the man. I was tired of traveling the roads alone, living out of motels while I did it. I had joined the military at eighteen because I hadn't wanted to go to college to follow in my father's footsteps. I joined to see the world, and what I saw was a few countries with a lot of goddamned sand. When I left after my last tour was over, I picked my bike up at my parents' house and traveled the US for a while. Now I was ready for a place to plant myself and build a life.

"What the hell, I'm in," I answered. Really, what did I have to lose?

Wild Bill pulled his phone out and texted, then laid it down on his desk. He stood, walked around his desk, and

CM Books, LLC

stuck his hand out to me. We shook hands just as there was a knock at the door, and Wild Bill yelled, "Enter." The door opened and in walked Hawk, Keg, Crank, Tram, and Pinch. Congrats were said and hands offered in welcome. When it was done, Wild Bill took his seat as did the rest of us and he began informing me of the *more* that Haven was. Well, at least some of the members.

That had been over three years ago as I recalled, sitting on the cot in the cell I was placed in the night before when I was brought into the correctional center through the back entrance. Parts had been played when I was sent here two years ago, it had worked then, and it needed to continue to work. Eyes were still on us, and every part had to be played to perfection.

Grinding metal sounded, and the cell door slid open. "Ready to go, Harris." I nodded and stepped out of the eight by ten room I had been placed in. Men who had been there a long time stood at their cell doors to watch as I passed by on my trek to out-process. Some would dream of their turn while others, their time served would only come after their death, but each lived vicariously through those who were released.

The hallway leading out seemed longer than it had been when I'd first been here. How anyone lived closed in behind the concrete walls was something I hoped never to have to experience on a permanent basis. The first time I was brought here it had been raining, this day, the sun's heat felt good when it hit my face as we stepped out the main doors onto the sidewalk that would lead me to the last thing keeping me behind the prison walls. We stopped in front of the last barrier, the guard signaled and flashed his ID badge in front of the camera and a short minute later the gate slid open, and I walked through. It might have been stupid, but I breathed easier as if I really was breathing fresh air for the first time, which could have been, compared to where I had actually come from less than forty-eight hours earlier.

I saw Alex Long, Haven's attorney, standing on the other side of the fence. As I stepped toward him, I heard the gate snap back into place and the sound of locks being engaged behind me. If I never heard the sound again, it would be too soon.

"Moose, I swear you are even bigger than the last time I saw you," Alex said, and we shook hands. Alex handled any and everything the club needed to be taken care of legally, and he was paid well for his services too.

"You know, gotta stay in shape for what we do," I said, and Alex chuckled.

I hadn't been a patched member of Haven very long before this plan was put into motion and I headed out for two years to a couple of different deserts unable to even come back to visit my brothers. I knew they had been notified of my return, so I wasn't too surprised when we reached the parking lot to see a group of men standing in front of their motorcycles. Everything had to be played out to make it believable.

"Goddamn, brother, being away from us did a body good, your ass is cut more now," Hawk said, and slapped my back as we bumped fists.

14

"I figured your right arm would be bigger than your left, but I guess even in the desert you were able to find a woman," Crank said, and the others laughed as I moved from each to receive pats on the back and handshakes.

"Glad you're back, brother. I missed that ugly face," Pinch said.

"Not more than me, man," I answered.

"Prez said to tell you a cold one would be waiting for ya at the clubhouse," Keg said.

"Well, then let's move out, we are burning daylight if we're making it back to the clubhouse tonight," Crank said, slapped my back like the others, and turned toward his bike.

"Hold up. I'm riding in the cage. I'm not riding bitch back to the fucking clubhouse," I said, and that was when I noticed my bike as the men parted and chuckled. Brothers, they always had my back. They knew I'd want to have the wind in my face and sitting in the truck for the ride home would have been brutal.

"Give us some credit, Moose. We had one of the Prospects ride it up; Latch is riding back with Alex."

"Damn, I love you guys in the most non-sexual way there is," I said as I walked to my bike and threw my leg over and straddled it. Nothing felt better than when my ass hit the seat.

"Fuck, thank God. I was worried we might have to watch bending over around you for a while if there weren't any women around," Hawk said and mounted his bike.

CM Books, LLC

"Yeah, yeah, 'cause your hairy asses are something I would have thought of every night if there wasn't." I laughed as I got comfortable on my bike.

"If you boys are done kissin' and shit, can we get on the road? Who knows what has gone on at the club while we've been gone," Crank said and started his bike.

"Prez will fill you in when we get back, Moose. He wanted to catch you up himself," Keg said and did the same as Crank. The rest followed suit, and as we pulled out of the lot, the pickup with Alex and the Prospect fell in behind us.

The ride was long, but I hadn't minded it one bit. We reached the clubhouse, and when we pulled into the lot, there were bikes lined up, filling most of the space. Some of the brothers were outside and came to greet me when I dismounted my bike. Others greeted me when I walked into the clubhouse. It had definitely not been what I had expected.

As we made our way through the crowd, I had half dressed women hugging and telling me to look them up when I was ready. Shit, it wasn't going to be a hardship acting as if I'd been two years without pussy when I watched a brunette's ass shake as she passed by. Her short skirt barely covered the cheeks of her ass, and the thought of what I would like to do to it made me smile.

"'Bout fucking time. I thought you might have kept on riding instead of coming back to Haven, Moose," Wild Bill said as he came up beside me and slapped me so hard on the back that I imagined if I had a smaller build, I would be kissing the floor.

"Nah, Prez, this is fucking home," I answered. Keg had been right, the Prez handed me a cold beer, and I cracked it open and took a swallow, savoring the taste as it slid over my tongue and down my throat.

"Before you start getting comfortable and going in search of a woman, let's step into my office and chat a minute. You boys' cuts are in there too where you left them," Wild Bill said and headed in the direction of his office. He knew we'd follow.

When we walked in, Tram was already there, we shook hands, and he welcomed me back. He hadn't made the trip to the prison with the others. When he stepped back, that was when I noticed the new patch on his cut.

"Congrats, brother," I said as I slapped the palm of my hand on the patch, so he would know what I was talking about. His new patch showed he held the secretary position in the club.

"Thanks, brother. Good to have you back," Tram said, then walked over and picked up the cuts that laid neatly on the table in the corner. As he passed each brother, he handed them each their cuts, leaving him with one. The last one in his hand, he gave over to Wild Bill, who took it and leaned his butt against the front of his desk while the others put their cuts on. They hadn't worn them to the prison, which I guessed I had been too excited about riding to notice.

A smile slid across my face when I noticed that Tram wasn't the only one wearing an extra patch on his cut.

CM Books, LLC

Hawk's held the VP patch, Pinch's held Treasurer, Keg's held Enforcer, and Crank's held Road Captain.

"Damn, shit looks good on you guys. I'm so damn happy to see you with those patches, brothers." And I was. I had left right before Stone, the old VP, had gone on the run after Wild Bill found out he had been leading a planned coup of sorts for the club.

He'd been the one who had set me up for the assault that was supposed to land me in prison. When Roach had overheard the plan between Stone and Jacks, we'd decided to let it play out and see if they would lead us to others in the club who were working against us. I'd been heading back to the club after visiting my folks, and when I was two towns away Haven, I was pulled over by a sheriff. Thinking it was just for harassment because I was wearing my cut, but imagine my surprise when he ran my driver's license and informed me I was wanted in connection with an assault. I'd supposedly beat a man at a bar after he walked up to confront me while I was outside on the side of the place fucking his wife. I was hauled to county lockup without any proof of the incident other than the word of the man and his wife.

The man and his wife testified against me. If the club hadn't of had some contacts of our own, the prison I just left would have actually been my home for two years. Instead, I only passed through the doors for strictly show and headed to my first desert stop to help with a situation that could have killed thousands of people if the ones behind the planned attack would have been allowed to initiate their plans.

"Yeah, the club has been getting a new and much-needed change in its leadership. We still haven't cleared Haven of all the trash, but we will. You know how it is, always more than one or two cockroaches." We chuckled, and then Wild Bill continued. "Moose, the Wyatts were given new identities once they came clean with who hired them. It was made to look like they had packed up prior to your arrest and then after they testified against you, they were taken out of the courthouse and given a fresh start. Stone was behind it; he was also behind the failed attempts to set up some of the others who wouldn't join with him in trying to take over the club. They tried to get rid of Keg, but he found the coke they planted in his saddlebags before the cops had a chance to be involved, same with Hawk, Pinch, Crank, and a few of the others. Keg, he was going to have to get rid of before he could have taken the presidency away from me, him being my son and all. Stone and his group seemed to focus on the younger men in the club. He figured if he could get you guys to go along, he would not only have the numbers but thought he could outsmart you boys. That was his mistake; young doesn't necessarily mean that someone can't equate to loyalty, smarts, or the ability to see through another's bullshit. The older members would have gone along with him only because they have been in this club their whole lives and wouldn't have wanted to move on, nor could they have physically taken Stone and his bunch on. Shock, Freak, and Roach, they've been with Haven back to

19

my old man's youth and subsequently to his takeover of Prez from my grandfather. Haven has history, it may not be the best, but the club has held together over time. I, for one, would like to see its future continue and it is going to be with you men." The others and I nodded in agreement to Wild Bill's words.

"You got my loyalty, Prez. You've always had it from the first day I came to Haven, that's not changed, and I will support my brothers who have stepped up into the officer positions now," I said, and the others just looked at me and grinned, which I had no clue why. I'd been a Prospect with Hawk, Keg, and the others. Each of us had joined Haven at roughly the same time and around a year before I was so called imprisoned, we had been full members in Haven.

Wild Bill stood from the leaned position he had on the desk and walked to stand in front of me. "I never doubted that, Moose." He held the cut that he had in his hand out to me and nodded for me to take it. When I held it up, looking at it more closely, it was mine from before I had left. My brows creased as I looked at the addition to it and when I looked back at Prez, he grinned.

"Haven was lucky the day you join us. And the team became complete that day too. I'd be honored to have you at my back on a permanent basis. You'd been there before just like the others, but we had to hold off on getting rid of Stone out of the club leadership because we were hoping he would lead us to who he was working for. The fucker wanted the club, but I think that was to be his payoff for helping someone else, a bigger player. After you left and went overseas with Grayson's team as cover for your supposed jail term, that was when we were going to grab Stone and Jacks. Use other means to get the info we needed, but they went on the run. Someone had to have known we were close to getting him and gave him a heads up." I was left speechless as I slid the cut over my t-shirt. "You along with this bunch are going to help me get this club back to the strong club it was before Stone infected it, and as far as our other jobs, we get the best of both worlds, doing things we like, and on our terms.

"Welcome back, Moose, to Haven and to the team," Wild Bill said as he shook my right hand while I ran my left hand over the patch that showed I was Haven's new Sergeant at Arms.

CM Books, LLC

# Chapter One

## Moose

Keg pulled the van around the back of the clubhouse and parked as close as he could get to the concrete stairs that led down to the entrance of the club's basement. I opened the passenger door, got out, slammed it shut, and before I moved away, I bent from side to side the stretch out my frame. I hated fucking cages. It probably had to do with the fact there weren't many vehicles built with a guy my size in mind.

"Damn, I'm beat. Let's get these two inside," Keg said from the back of the van.

"Yeah, lock them up, and then we can go upstairs to the bar. I don't know about you, but I could use a cold one, and a couple of aspirin. We should have gagged those assholes before we left Black Hawk. Sad it only took fifty miles of their whining and bitching to give me a damn headache." I rubbed my temples and moved beside Keg.

CM Books, LLC

He opened the rear doors to the van, which revealed the two men bungee-corded back to back as they sat in the middle, each of their ankles zip-tied along with their wrists.

Keg and I reached in, unhooked the bungee cord, and we each grabbed an arm of one of the men. Both tried to jerk out of our hands, probably due to the gunshot wounds they were both sporting, compliments of the men from Black Hawk MC.

After we had them standing, the door to the basement opened, and Shock walked up the concrete steps. When he reached us, he looked the two men up and down and spit on the ground in front of them.

"They give you boys any trouble?" Shock asked just as Keg cut the zip-tie on Jacks' feet and he kicked out just missing Keg's head. Before Keg could react, Shock moved forward and coldcocked Jacks, jarring his head to the side. When I looked down at Shock's hand, I noticed for the first time he wore brass knuckles.

"Come prepared, did ya?" I chuckled as Jacks moaned behind the duct tape across his mouth. I bent down, sliced the tie on Stone's ankles, and stood back up. I looked at Stone who had stiffened and was staring at Shock, a little fear shining in his eyes. He should fear Shock; a lot of people did. He and Freak were the oldest members of the club. Both were in their sixties, and both had been in POW camps in the Vietnam War. Some of the things that I'd heard were done to them would have broken lesser men. They each carried the mental and physical abuse they had endured as a badge for the times.

24

"Prepared keeps you alive. Besides, didn't want the snakes to slither away." Shock pulled off the brass knuckles and placed them in his pocket as he started to walk behind Keg who dragged Jacks down the steps and through the door.

Stone tried to talk behind his own tape as I led him and followed Shock. When we walked down the short hallway, it opened up into a large room. We called it the common room. It held a TV, a couple of sofas, and a few chairs. Off to one side were stairs that led up to the kitchen of the main part of the clubhouse, and under the steps was another doorway that led to a soundproof room with a couple of cells. Not that we kept people prisoner every day, but it was there if we needed it, like now.

The sounds of boots made us turn toward the stairs, and we watched as Wild Bill and Hawk made their way down into the room.

"Prez," Keg and I said at the same time as we led the men under the stairs and into the room that held the cells with Wild Bill and Hawk behind us. Shock opened the first cell, and Keg ripped the tape off Jacks' mouth and pushed him in. I did the same with Stone once Shock closed the door to Jacks' cell and opened the other one.

"You goddamn fuckers, when I get out of here, I'm going to kill every damn one of you," Stone bitched as he rubbed his hand over his mouth where the tape had been ripped away.

"Wallace, long time no see. Awful mouthy considering," Wild Bill said and stood in front of the door to the cell. Stone stared back at the Prez and sneered.

"That stupid cunt, I should have gotten rid of her with her mother," Stone said, and I reached through the bars, grabbed him by his neck, and pulled him against the bars.

Wallace Stone had always been an asshole who never knew when to keep his mouth shut. Wild Bill had sent Sami and Carly to Black Hawk territory to be protected while he worked on getting the club cleaned up. It had brought an alliance with Stroker and his club, but it had cost Wild Bill time with his daughter, Sami, then his granddaughter too when Sami had given birth to Ally. It hadn't been easy at the beginning for Sami and Carly to be away, but now both were settled in the town of Shades Valley. Sami was the ol' lady to Speed who was one of the enforcers, and if the actions of Crusher, the new President was anything to go by, Carly would soon be his ol' lady.

"You want that tape back on your damned mouth? When we are done with you, you're gonna wish Crusher would have finished you off. Underestimated his club, didn't you? You have always thought you were smarter than everyone else. But you're done, Stone, you just haven't realized it yet," I said as I released the hold on his neck and shoved him back. He stumbled briefly but didn't fall. I looked over at Jacks who hadn't said a word and saw that he was looking toward the door. I looked over my shoulder, and Freak stood in the doorway with a smirk on his face.

CM Books, LLC

"Welcome to the party, boys. Shock and I have been waiting for you," Freak said and stepped in the room.

"Ah, Freak, they may give us what we need, and then yours and Shock's services won't be needed," Wild Bill said and Hawk, Keg, and I chuckled when Freak frowned at the Prez.

"You mean I let Spitfire and Rattler go hungry for nothin', Prez?" I watched Jacks' eyes go wide at Freak's words, and it took everything in me not to burst out laughing. Those damn snakes were Freak's babies; there would be no way he would let them go hungry. He and Shock were the only members who had permanent rooms in the clubhouse and even with the spare rooms upstairs, they chose to occupy the only two bedrooms in the basement.

Wild Bill had said it gave them a place to go when the noise got too loud around the clubhouse or their own safe haven when the past surfaced to remind them they couldn't lock those memories away forever. PTSD, post-traumatic stress disorder, was the medical term everyone liked to use; Freak and Shock, though, referred to it as the price they paid for being young and serving their country. Something they would go through again if they were needed.

"Bullshit, you ain't going to do anything, old man," Stone said as he stared down Freak. "This is why the club should've been mine, you and your fuck buddy would have been the first to go."

Even with the whispers that were heard through the club, mainly due to the men not having old ladies or being seen with any women, but no one in the club had witnessed

27

them acting anything other than the close friends they were. Frankly, who gave two shits, sexual preference belonged to the individual. Not one man in the club, including myself, could say the two weren't the epitome of what brotherhood was about. Shock and Freak stood strong. And if anyone thought to write the two off as just old men, it would be their funeral.

"Cocksucker, have you been using too much of your own product or soaking your liver with booze? Don't let the gray hair fool ya. We could kill you six different ways before you even clued in on what the fuck was happening to you. So keep thinking you would have ever controlled Haven, 'cause I don't consider five minutes to be a leadership term, and that would have been the amount of time you'd held the prez position," Shock said and moved to stand by Freak.

"We're going to get some things set up for when you need us. Those two are going down just like the other two that shot Carly. They talked big too, but in the end, they were the ones standing in soiled pants, and we were the ones with the info," Freak said, and then he and Shock walked out. Christ, the two of them were as crazy as hell.

"You're one stupid fucker, Stone," Hawk said and shook his head.

"Well, look who speaks. Heard Wild Bill allowed some of the young pups to move up. Think they're going to help you keep your position and the club. Please, you hold that spot only because of your old man. If I had gotten more support from some of the pussy members, you would be gone just like your dad." Stone moved back and sat down on

CM Books, LLC

the cot when he finished with his little speech geared toward the Prez. I watched Stone's and Jacks' eyes, their mannerisms, every twitch of the muscles on their faces. It would tell a story, at least if you knew what to look for. I'd always been good at reading people. When I was in the military, they tagged me as a profiler because I could take information, pictures, anything else about a subject, and piece it together until it felt as though I was in on the person's thoughts, enabling me to map his/her movements. Having them both here, allowing me to monitor them personally... I didn't think it would take long for us to bust any others who were involved with Stone but trying to lay low under the radar.

I ran his rant over in my head, and something in his statement hit me. When I zoned back into my surroundings, Wild Bill was stepping even closer to the cage door.

"You don't know what the word loyalty means, dumbass. But I will say, the stupidest move my dad made was allowing you and your," Prez fanned his hand in Jacks' direction, "goddamn punk ass boys to move into any leadership positions with Haven. I could stand here and argue with you back and forth over shit that has gone down, but why waste the breath, you're inside that cell, and I'm standing out here." Wild Bill turned his back on Stone and Jacks and faced us. "Let's go upstairs, have a beer. I've changed my mind on giving them the opportunity to answer our questions without a little incentive. They can answer to Shock and Freak." Prez headed for the door and Hawk, Keg, and I turned to follow.

"Hey, what about our wounds and some food!" Stone yelled.

I heard the clinking noise as either Stone or Jacks hit their cell door, then looked over my shoulder at Keg who was behind me and the last one exiting the room. He stopped before pulling the door shut.

"Why? Not like you're going to get a chance for the wounds to kill you or even a chance for starvation to work a number on you." Keg looked at me and winked before he pulled the door shut.

I chuckled as we headed toward the stairs. Once upstairs with a cold beer in hand, I shared my thoughts on Stone as we gathered around the bar in the corner.

"Prez, when your dad was shot in that deal gone bad, who was on the run with him?"

"Why? What are thinking, Moose?"

"Stone's statement about you being gone like your dad. We know he killed Carly's mom by making it look like an overdose. Are you sure the bastard didn't shoot your pops?" Wild Bill frowned at my words and was quiet in thought as if remembering that time.

"Stone, Creeper, Jacks, and a couple of the other members went on that run with my dad. Dad had gone because it was a new contact and partnership, and they wanted to meet with the president of the club. A matter of fact, the other two who went were prospects." I could tell Wild Bill was trying to put all the pieces together and knew the moment he did.

"What did you remember, Prez?" The others and I waited for him to speak.

"Never thought about this but the two prospects, Boots and Mic, were in a fatal crash a week later. And they just so happened to be out on an errand for Stone when they were run off the road because a pickup was passing an eighteen wheeler and was in their lane. They swerved to the right to miss it, but their tires hit the soft shoulder and sent them over the incline, flipping the bikes, and they were pronounced dead at the scene. The trucker had pulled over and ran back to try to help, and the pickup just kept going. The driver was able to give a description of the truck and a plate number to the cops, but the plate had been stolen off a car from California, and the truck itself had been found the next day, abandoned and burnt out, leaving no prints to run for the driver. The cops had thought it had to do with a group that was jacking cars, breaking them down, and selling the parts, but figured they burnt that one out because of the accident and deaths of the two men. What you are thinking is more logical. Just something else to get to the bottom of with Stone because I wouldn't put anything past the asshole."

"Prez, I also think it goes deeper than just wanting to be president of Haven. Stone stayed on the run for several years. He had to be getting money from somewhere to live and stay hidden until just recently. That tells me his cash flow was cut off, and since club life is all he knows, he was heading back here. Him going after Carly, well, in his mind, he saw her as the beginning of his downfall, even as

31

misguided as that sounds." Just as I finished my theory, the music went up and the club party picked up. Prez looked around and then leaned in so we could hear him over the music.

"I'm heading home; we can go over more of this tomorrow. Hawk, make sure Stone and Jacks get some damn food. As much as I might want them dead, I would much rather get some answers," Wild Bill said and set his beer bottle down on the bar.

"Sure thing, Prez. See you tomorrow." Wild Bill nodded to us.

"If you party too hard, stay in the rooms upstairs. Don't want a call one of you are dead or locked up because your ass rode drunk." Prez slapped Keg on the back as he passed him headed for the door.

"Your dad has worked hard to bring this club back, Keg. It sure will be nice when it's a hundred percent healthy.

"Agree, brother. I can't remember a day since he has been Prez that he hasn't had to worry about something going on with this club," Keg said and took a swig of beer.

"Hopefully, we can get it done this time around," Crank said, and we all agreed.

"Well, let's enjoy tonight because I have a feeling that starting tomorrow—shit is going to get real," I said and looked at each of my brothers.

"Your gut talking, Moose?" Tram asked.

"Yeah, and it's telling me things are going to change. I just hope for the better." I walked off, leaving them with my last thought on the matter. At least for the night.

32

# Chapter Two

## Katie

"Dr. Stevens, you have a call on line three," Sandy, the desk nurse, said as I walked up and laid my last patient's file on the counter.

"Thanks, Sandy." I picked up the phone and pushed the button for the call that was on hold and said, "Dr. Stevens."

"Katie?"

"Dad, you never call me at the hospital. Is everything okay with Mom?" Paul Stevens, my dad, never called me at work. Shit, the man hardly called me at all unless my mother needed her prescriptions filled. Mary Stevens was diagnosed bipolar ten years ago, and it had been rough for all of us. She would go from the cheerful mother and wife to the depressed woman who couldn't even get dressed. The physician to finally take the time to get her meds correct worked with me at the hospital. It didn't matter how many times I told them that they needed to call his office; they

CM Books, LLC

ignored me. So now, I was left contacting his office to have them call in her prescriptions to the local pharmacy by their house. It was less traumatic that way.

"Kathryn, I don't have time for you to get an attitude with me," my dad said, and I rolled my eyes. The man never had time for anything or anyone that wasn't one of his precious clients.

"I am busy, Dad, if not for Mom, why did you call?" I flipped through the chart of the next patient waiting to be seen while I listened to my dad talk.

"Katie, you need to be more diligent with your surroundings. And if anyone comes around and mentions knowing me or makes you uncomfortable, call me." My dad's voice took a tone that I had never heard before. Worry? Fear?

"Something going on I should know about, Dad? And why would I call you if something were to happen? What aren't you telling me, dammit?"

"Nothing, Katie. Just concerned for you since you took that job. I know the quality of patients who come there are..." I closed my eyes and counted to ten at his words. He never failed to get his digs in because I didn't go into private practice so I could attend to the wealthy instead of the poor and working class who came to General Hospital for their care. I frequently wondered when he turned into such a snobbish person.

"Okay, Dad, I gotta go. Patients to see. Tell Mom I said hi."

"Just remember what I said, Kathryn. Bye." Before I got a chance to return the bye, I had a dial tone sounding in my ear. I hung up the phone and headed to the exam room where my next patient sat waiting, the phone call with my dad easily forgotten.

I moved the curtain aside and walked into the cubical to find a large man sitting on the exam table wearing jeans, a black t-shirt, and boots. His dirty blond hair pulled back in a ponytail and his brown eyes looking me over. When his eyes raised to look me in the eyes, he wore a smirk on his face.

"Hello, Mr. Mizer. I'm Dr. Stevens. Your vitals are normal. Let's see about getting that cut on your arm stitched. It says here you were working on your bike and sliced your forearm open."

His arm rested on the portable work table, and I began removing the gauze the nurse had wrapped around the arm to stifle the bleeding after cleaning the wound. The man never flinched even when the gauze pulled in a few spots from being stuck in the drying blood.

"Nice, soft touch there, doc. You got great hands. How about when you get off, I pick you up and I can take you for a ride on my bike, and you can run those great hands over other areas of my body."

Great, it's not like I've never been hit on, but usually, they were a little less creepy when they made advances. Not this guy, he said it and the smirk never left his face.

"Mr. Mizer, sorry, but I don't go out with patients, even when they ask me with such class." That statement received a change in his demeanor. He stiffened on the table,

35

and when I looked up from his arm, the smirk was gone, replaced with his lips pressed together and his jaw clenched as if he was gritting his teeth.

The area had already been numbed by the nurse who did the initial clean. I rolled over the table with the supplies I would need to stitch the man up. Once I began, the man sat quietly, and he hadn't even replied to my last comment. As I stitched the wound, I had my suspicions that it wasn't from working on his bike, the pattern of the slice looked more like it was from a jagged-edged knife.

"Mr. Mizer, are you sure someone didn't cut you? The wound is more precise than if you just hooked the skin on something."

"I told you how it was done. You callin' me a liar, bitch."

"Sir, there is no need for that kind of language. I asked a question. It is my job. I am for patching you up, no matter how you received the wound..." Mr. Mizer got ready to speak, and I held up my hand to stop him, "so you might want to cut the name calling, considering the one patching you up can use a knife a helluva lot better than the person who did this to you." I tied off the last stitch and set the tools down. My words had nothing to do with being scared but more to do with not showing fear. It hadn't taken me long after I started working in the ER to figure that out.

What had surprised me was the reaction from the man. He hadn't gotten pissed off, he laughed and looked between the nurse who entered and me, then said, "Feisty, that is a good trait."

CM Books, LLC

I refused to go back and forth with the man, so I wrapped the forearm again with clean gauze. Informed him of the 'taking care' portion of dealing with the wound. And then I walked out after handing him a copy of the cleaning instructions and telling him to either come back to the ER or see his regular physician in fourteen days to have the stitches removed or before if he noticed any redness or swelling around the wound.

At the nurses' station, I signed off on several charts and grabbed the next one of the patient who was next in line to be seen. I turned the corner just as Mr. Mizer was heading out.

"Doc?" I stopped and turned when he spoke.

"Yes?"

"Tell your father, Mr. Kosnoff says hello." He started to walk away.

"What are you talking about? How do you know my dad?"

The man laughed and as the doors to the outside opened and he walked through, he said over his shoulder, "Just give him the message, he'll understand." The doors closed behind him, and I stood there and stared until Suzy said my name. I turned to her, and she frowned.

"Is everything okay, Dr. Stevens?" she asked.

"Yeah, I just... I just thought I forgot something," I said and looked down at the chart in my hand, then back to her. "I will be in exam room eight." I left it at that and walked away. I wouldn't be calling my dad as he asked

CM Books, LLC

before. No, as soon as my shift ended, it would be handled in person.

⚘

When my shift ended at seven the next morning, I headed straight to my parents' house for the sole purpose of catching my dad before he headed into his office. By the time I drove across town and pulled into the driveway, it was ten minutes till eight.

Before I reached the front door, it was opened and my mother stood in the doorway. "Kathryn, what brings you by so early?"

"Did I miss Dad already?" I asked and watched my mother look over her shoulder before she answered.

"No, he hasn't left yet; he is in his office down the hall," she whispered.

"What is going on, Mom? Why are you whispering?" I frowned and waited for her to answer and once again watched her look over her shoulder before she spoke.

"I'm not sure. Your father won't tell me but, Kathryn, he has been nervous and jumpy for a while now. He hasn't been into the office for three days. He called them and told them he was under the weather, but for each of those days he has been in his office here going through papers." Mary Stevens didn't need any added stress with her condition, but I knew she was feeling it because of the way she was wringing her hands as she talked.

We moved out of the doorway, and I closed the door behind me. "I'll go see him and see if I can get him to talk about what is going on. It's not like him to take time off from the office or his precious clients." I left my mother standing in the hall and walked toward my father's office door. I knocked and received no answer, but it could have been because he didn't hear me for the sound of the shredder I heard being used on the other side of the door. I turned the handle, opened the door, and walked in to find my father standing by his industrial shredder with a stack of papers in one arm as he fed the machine.

"Dad!" I said loudly, startling him, and he whipped around to face me.

"What are you doing here?"

"Nice to see you too, Dad. I hear you are under the weather and haven't been into work. Funny, you didn't mention *that* when you called me. What is going on? And who the hell is Mr. Kosnoff?" I watched the change in his expression from surprise to what resembled fear.

"How do you know Mr. Kosnoff, Katie? Stay away from him. He is not someone you want to know." He walked to his desk and laid the papers down, then looked at me. "Well?"

"A patient I took care of in the ER dropped the name. So here I am, like you wanted, notifying you."

"I told you to call and let me know. Now you have. I will call Mr. Kosnoff and take care of everything. I just want you to be aware of what is going on around you, that's all." My dad never did anything that wasn't calculated and planned ahead of time, reworked six more times to make sure it came out the same every time. His behavior was so weird, and if I thought back, it had been a little off-kilter for some time. This just happened to be more extreme.

At one time, my dad and I had the typical father/daughter relationship. If I had to pinpoint when that changed, I would say when I decided to go into medicine and not the law as he had wanted. When he finally accepted that I wasn't going to be a lawyer but a doctor instead, I was interning at General, which started his disapproval all over again. The last couple of years had been nothing but him badgering me because I refused to give in to his meddling. Unfortunately for him, I was over the age of where a daughter gave a shit about her father's approval, especially when it was only given when I did as he wanted.

"Yeah, that is what you said but how about you actually tell me the truth about what is going on? Why are you shredding papers? Why are you missing work? And again, who is Mr. Kosnoff?" I knew from the look on his face he wasn't going to give in that easily, neither was I. "Before you give me some bullshit that you think I will buy, let's skip that part. And if you don't come clean, I will go by the offices and ask Mr. Harris." I stood there and watched my father's shoulders slump. He pulled the desk chair out and sat, letting out a breath. He motioned to the chair in front of the desk for me to sit. Once I was seated, he began to talk.

"Please don't interrupt until I am done, Katie. If you do, I may not be able to finish." I nodded my head, and he continued, "In the last ten years with the introduction of e-trading, my clientele dropped at the brokerage firm, causing

CM Books, LLC

my annual income to drop substantially because of it. With my knowledge in the market, I started dealing in high-risk stock and selling off when the price increased to supplement the loss in my income. The problem was that I didn't have the cash flow to do this, so I used the monies from some of the clients I still had. Everything went well until one purchase of stock in a pharmaceutical company that had a test drug with great success getting ready to come on the market, only waiting for FDA approval. I would have made millions and been able to put the initial monies back into my client's fund account. Two days before the approval, it was announced the pharmaceutical company had lied about some of the side effects, and the FDA postponed approval for further testing. The stock plummeted, and the money I invested was lost.

"The money belonged to Alexi Viktor Kosnoff, owner and CEO of Kosnoff shipping, an international company with offices in Vladivostok, Russia, Vancouver, Canada, and Seattle, Washington. I cashed in everything I had, plus what I had in savings but it wasn't enough. The jest is that Kosnoff found out and instead of turning me in, well, I cut a deal with the devil. It started as laundering money by setting up bogus trade accounts, and after a couple of years, I had paid back the amount I had lost, but by then Kosnoff owned me. He is into a lot of things, Katie, drugs, guns, human trafficking. I wanted out, but he threatened your mom and you if I didn't continue. He even has deals with a motorcycle club, using them to run the drugs and guns. Something happened there with one of the bikers, he fucked up and

CM Books, LLC

cost Kosnoff money. The club has caught the man who was essentially selling them out, and Kosnoff still has a hand in the club, but I don't know who that is. He still gets information through them." I didn't know the man that sat in front of me and talked. He wasn't the man I had grown up around.

"If you are still doing his bidding, why is he sending bikers to my work to give you messages?" I had a bad feeling as I waited for him to answer.

"I was in charge of the yearly audits at the firm, so I always hired the company that came in. The one I used was bought and paid for by Kosnoff, covering up anything that might look suspicious and draw the attention of the SEC until this year. Louis hired a new company for the audit after he came into my office to get a file, I had stepped out for just a minute to check with one of the junior brokers about a new client he had brought on board. I left a file out that no one was supposed to see, and Louis saw the motorcycle's club name and flipped through the file. He told me later, after hiring the auditing company, that if there was anything I needed to come clean about I had until the audit was done. After that, well, he hoped I didn't end up in jail.

"I panicked and have been shredding anything tying me to Kosnoff. I don't know why; it isn't like it can't be traced another way. Anyway, with this fuck up, Kosnoff wants me to get Louis to switch the auditing company back to the one he has on payroll. Katie, I can't go to jail."

"What in your mind told you this shit would be a good idea? I'm not talking your tie to Kosnoff. I'm talking using the man's money to begin with. And jail, sorry for what you have done, but you should go." I didn't know the man in front of me anymore.

"You don't understand, Katie."

"There is nothing to understand, you did illegal shit, and as far as I am concerned, what you get, you deserve."

"That may be, but Kosnoff won't stop with just me. You and your mother are in danger too."

"Because of you and your damn greed! What the fuck does a motorcycle club have to do with an international shipping company in the first place? Drugs, guns, what the fuck have you gotten involved in? And why would Louis know anything about a bike club in the first place?"

"One member of the club was trying to take over, and he cut some deal with Kosnoff. They had already been running drugs and guns for him. I told you that. I wasn't involved in that part, just the money and bogus trade accounts. For Louis, well, Katie, Linc is part of the club."

Linc. I would be lying if I said I didn't think of him often, but I did make an effort not to, it just never worked too well. I even avoided him when he came to town to visit his folks. I'd missed him when he left me behind, his excuse to me had been an easy way for him not to hurt my feelings. He was my first and not easily forgotten, but I didn't need a neon sign to say he moved on without me.

"So, Linc took a turn in his life, and that has what to do with me? Nothing, just like I meant nothing to him when he dumped me to move on." My father's head dropped, and he broke eye contact. Well damn, that wasn't a good sign.

43

CM Books, LLC

# Chapter Three

## Moose

The buzzing of my cell had me cussing. I reached for it without even opening my eyes. "Yo!"

"Really, Linc, that is how you answer your phone?" I inwardly groaned and wished I had looked at the caller ID before answering.

"Hey, Dad. How are you and Mom doing?" The overconsumption of beer last night left me sleeping in one of the rooms upstairs at the clubhouse. Throw in the time I spent fucking one of the hang-arounds, and I might have had three hours of sleep, tops. I moved the chick's arm that was slung over my chest, she moaned and rolled over on her back, her bare breasts revealed as the sheet slipped to her waist. As I sat up on the side of the bed, I ran my hand over the mounds and tweaked her nipples. Instant reaction to my touch had them hardening into peaks and eliciting another moan as she arched her back in sleep seeking more. My dick, as if it hadn't had enough action, hardened wanting to give

CM Books, LLC

her exactly what she was asking for. Maybe I'd get to that after I got off the phone with my dad.

"We're fine, son. But, Linc, there's a problem at the firm. It involves Paul." I listened to my dad and couldn't believe the shit I was hearing.

"You know that shit has been going on for over five fucking years. I can't talk about club business, Dad. But I'll give you what I can. We recently obtained... something we hope will be able to give us some much-needed answers. You know not everyone here at the club are involved, right?" My dad had always been understanding with every decision I had ever made with my life, whether he agreed with it or not, I only got the support, never the negative.

"Linc, son, that never entered my mind, not once. You may not have wanted to follow in my footsteps, but that has nothing to do with the man you have grown into. You reached out and grabbed what you wanted in life, not what others expected out of you. That, Linc, means more to your mother and me than the fact you wear leathers and ride a motorcycle or even camouflage."

"Glad to hear. Does Katie know about any of this?" I looked over my shoulder to make sure the woman was still asleep as I grabbed my boxers and headed into the bathroom and shut the door.

"I haven't talked to her, son. I don't know." I faced the mirror and rubbed my hand over my face as my dad continued. "Son, I haven't asked what happened between the two of you. I figured you would tell me when you were ready. But, Linc, I was sure after you found your place and

CM Books, LLC

got settled, that you would come back for her. When you didn't, well, I didn't want to pry." His voice lowered as he continued, "She's never married. She isn't even seeing anyone. Katie avoids asking about you, and that is when I see her at all, she avoids your mother and me, too. I've been married to your mother for almost forty years, and I know when a man looks at a woman the way you did at her graduation, it isn't because you are indifferent about how you feel. It is more like knowing that what you are looking at is yours. I knew something was wrong when you didn't show up at Paul and Mary's house for Katie's party. But like I said, didn't want to pry."

"Thanks for not mentioning to them that you saw me there. Keep me posted, and I'll do some digging, see what else I can come up with. When I have anything, I'll be in touch." We said our goodbyes, and I hung up, turned around, and started the shower. Once it was heated, I stepped in and let the hot water pour over my head and down my back. As I leaned my hands against the wall, I closed my eyes and brought Katie's face up and pictured the last time I saw her.

She had her dark brown hair in a bun, and from where I stood, I saw her brown eyes sparkle as she received her diploma. She'd been beautiful as a sixteen-year-old girl, but as a young woman in her twenties, she was gorgeous and looked ready to take on the world. I'd come that day to claim her as mine, but instead, I walked away alone and tried not to look back at everything I was giving up.

47

Now, after I listened to my dad, it brought everything with her front and center that I had long ago locked away. Her laugh, her smile, the first time I kissed her, the night I took her virginity, even her face with tears running down when I said goodbye to her, to not only find a place for myself, but to build something to share with her. She had her dreams too, and I wanted her to finish growing up and fill them. I wanted no regrets for her or me when I claimed her as mine.

As I stepped out of the shower, dried off, and went into the bedroom to get dressed, the only thing running through my head was Kathryn Stevens had been mine since she was six years old and pushed me in the pool when I told her girls couldn't swim as good as boys.

I left the bedroom without a word to the woman in the bed, it might make me a dick, but to me, she and every other woman I'd bedded had only been to fill a need until I pulled my head out of my ass and went after what had always been mine.

First, Haven MC had to be cleared of its issues. Then I had a woman to claim. I had a feeling the first was going to be a helluva lot easier than the second.

When I walked into the kitchen of the clubhouse, I found Wild Bill sitting at the table drinking coffee. I went to the counter and poured a cup and joined him.

"You're lookin' a little rough around the edges." He smirked at me over the rim of the coffee cup before he took a drink. He seemed in a better mood than he'd left in last night.

"Yeah, yeah, Prez, laugh it up. My dad called me this morning, and after I tell you what he said, you won't find anything funny." He set the coffee cup down and sat up straight in his chair.

"Really, like shit couldn't get any worse than we have been dealing with."

"Maybe, but not in the way you think. Hell, I find the shit hard to believe, but my old man may have helped us and not even known it." I took a drink of my coffee and informed Wild Bill of everything my dad informed me of. He listened without a word until I was finished.

"Sonofabitch. Text the others and tell them to get their sorry asses in here for Church. And when you are done getting a hold of them, have Shock and Freak join us. I want some answers now, and that piece of shit in the basement is going to give them to me." He pushed back his chair, and on his way out of the kitchen, he yelled over his shoulder as I pulled out my phone, "I'll be in my office when they arrive. That's where we will meet."

Forty minutes later, Keg, Crank, Tram, Pinch, Hawk, and I sat in the Prez's office. And if we weren't preparing to talk about some serious shit when Shock and Freak walked in, I would have laughed. They would only sit in on the part of the meeting that concerned them, but anyone who knew them could tell they were out of their element as they took the two empty chairs at the table. With everyone present that needed to be there, our Prez started right in.

"Some stuff has been brought to my attention, and though I would love nothing better than to let Stone and Jacks sit down in those cells and sweat for a few days on what we are going to do to them, we need answers.

"Shock and Freak, you got any issues doing your thing?" Prez looked down the table at the two men.

"No problem at all, Prez," Freak answered first.

"Never liked that bastard. He was a brother and our VP, I would have done for him what I would do for any other brother in this club, but that didn't mean I had to like him. So now that he is out, I'm with Freak, got no problem taking care of business. Might need a new battery but we'll get the answers you need."

I could almost feel sorry for Stone and Jacks, almost. We'd heard some of the shit Stone had done to Shock and Freak back in the day and if he had pulled that shit after we joined, VP or not, he would have gone down. Roach told us about the worst one. One night after a club party, Stone, Jacks, and Creeper went to the basement after Shock and Freak had gone into their bedrooms and set off fireworks in the common area. Not only did the dumbasses almost catch the room on fire, but they also sent Shock and Freak into battlefield mode. The assholes thought it would only scare Shock and Freak. Instead, the men came out of their rooms in full battle gear, crawling on their bellies and firing into the room. Stone and his flunkies laughed as they ran upstairs when the gunfire started. Well, until a shot came through the floor missing Stone's foot by inches. Everyone at the clubhouse cleared out and three days passed before anyone stepped back into the clubhouse.

Wild Bill's dad had to grease quite a few palms to keep charges from being filed. Not to mention the repairs to the clubhouse, which he made Stone and his guys pay for it, and that only made their hatred for Shock and Freak grow.

"Whatever you need, let Moose know. One of us will be down when you are ready to start, then the questions can be asked. I would suggest Stone be first up. He will try to hold out, which will make Jacks wonder if Stone is throwing him under the bus. Jacks will break, but I'm not sure he knows everything. However, if we keep Jacks talking a while before he gets taken back to the cell, Stone will be sweating, and his second round should go so much smoother. He'll be more willing to share information.

"So, Shock, you and Freak get your toys ready, see if you need anything. We'll finish the meeting and then check with you to make sure you are ready." Shock and Freak stood and headed for the door without a word. When the door closed behind them, Wild Bill continued.

"I'm going to turn the meeting over to Moose, and he can tell you what his father found out. Once he's finished, we'll decide how to proceed." Everyone nodded in agreement, and then all eyes turned toward me.

I went over the information, and the guys listened just as Wild Bill had done earlier. When I finished, it seemed the other men were as shocked as I was about what Stone had been up to.

CM Books, LLC

"How did he know the account with Haven wasn't ours?" Hawk asked.

"He knew it was another account because he handles our brokerage fund personally. He is the one who gives us the list of stocks he thinks we should invest in, and then we vote on the ones we want to go with. Paul's account isn't under Haven, it's under Stone's name and listed him as VP of Haven MC. It brought up a red flag for my dad and he investigated a little, and that's where we are at right now," Hawk nodded in understanding as I spoke.

"Moose, we need to stay in touch with your dad, especially if he is going to monitor Paul's accounts to see if anything else pops up that we could use."

"You got it, Prez."

"Great. Now before we settle in downstairs, I wanted to tell you we have about a month before you boys leave on a job. I just received the paperwork today from General Patel, so let's get this wrapped up as quick as possible. It's time to get the club healthy and in good working order, and that means flushing the rest of the shit down the bowl. It's been a long time coming but cleaning up the club is finally in reach."

The last few years wasn't easy on any of us, but Wild Bill carried more weight on his shoulders through the adjustments and changes. Haven was started by his grandfather, and though the club leaned more toward illegal activity, they never failed to take care of their own. Then as the times changed and Wild Bill's father took over, Stone started slowly and quietly dividing the ranks until the club began to implode internally. By the time Wild Bill left the military and returned to Haven with his family, the club was no better than a street gang. Haven had a few good men leave doing that time because they were tired of putting up with all the crap.

When Wild Bill's father was killed, Stone thought he'd have enough support to take the club over. Instead, Wild Bill took his place at the head of the table. He hadn't known then that Stone was a snake in the grass. Once he started the internal cleanup, the pressure switched to Stone. The others and I joined Haven, paid our dues and worked our way up in the club, helping the club on its way.

It's been said you must fight the battles to win the war—well, hopefully, with the extermination of Stone and Jacks, Haven's war will be over and the club whole again.

While we sat at the table, we hashed out a plan, and when we finished, I was up first for Stone duty. The only thing running through my mind as I stood, *let the fun begin*.

CM Books, LLC

CM Books, LLC

# Chapter Four

## Moose

Jacks was sitting on the cot in his cell when I walked in the room. He lifted his head and stood when he noticed me.

"What the fuck is going on?" His voice panicky when he asked, telling me what I already knew. Shock and Freak had come for Stone.

"Ah, you decide it was time to talk now? It seems Stone did, too. He's telling Shock and Freak one hell of a story. I find it hard to believe you were actually that smart, not including that you had any friends outside the club. Especially friends with any kind of power. I mean seriously, Jacks, you're a follower. I don't think you could lead if you were the only man you had to direct. So forgive me if I don't buy you as having any friends with the pull Stone is giving away. Come on, Jacks, we both know you have your head up Stone's ass that if he stops quick enough, you'd need a neck brace."

I watched Jacks' face and saw exactly what I was looking for—belief that his pal was selling him out. Fuck, this might be easier than we originally thought. Shows Jacks as the weakest link, but I still would have never pegged him to go down this fast.

"Stone wouldn't give me up. You're lying." The paranoia had begun, and it would be what brought them both down.

"Sure, 'cause he is one trustworthy brother there. Standup guy who wouldn't think of stabbing anyone in the back if it would benefit him. What did he promise you, Jacks? Money, women, power? You are dumber than I thought if you think he has any plans sharing shit with you."

I watched his eyes, he wanted to talk but wasn't quite ready to let it out, so yeah, I'd leave him with something to think about until his turn was up with Shock and Freak.

"Heard Kosnoff was a smart businessman. Can't imagine he would leave two loose ends dangling in the wind. Well, what would I know? Maybe you and Stone are smarting than me." Jacks' eyes flashed. It was the response I wanted. I turned toward the door and opened it, and Mondo walked in carrying food. If I hadn't been paying close attention, I would have missed the slightest shift in his facial expression at the surprise of seeing me. Interesting.

"Oh, Moose, I didn't know you were down here. Where's the other piece of shit? I was told to bring down food for them." Mondo glanced at the empty cell beside Jacks' and then back to me.

"Just leave Stone's. He'll be back. Maybe." Mondo walked into the open cell and sat a plate down on the empty cot before sliding the extra plate through the slot in Jacks' cell door.

I stood just outside the door and watched Jacks take hold of the tray while purposely not looking at Mondo or saying a word to him. Even though his body language said, he love nothing better.

"Good to know," Mondo said, and I waited until Mondo walked out.

"Enjoy, Jacks, you'll up next," I said, then grabbed the door closing it behind me. It was time for me to see exactly what Shock and Freak were up to with Stone.

I moved to the end of the hall and pulled the key out for the door. It was made of heavy metal, soundproofed just like the rest of the room, and it had an automatic locking mechanism when it closed. The way to enter or exit was with a key, and the only members outside of leadership to have a key were Shock and Freak.

The door opened, and my first thought was, *damn, wished I hadn't eaten so much at lunch*. The room was going to need bleached and aired out by the time this was finished. The urine smell alone was strong, add body odor, and you had a volatile combo for your senses.

Stone was chained by his wrist to the ceiling; his feet barely would reach the floor if he dropped them. Stone had his legs bent at the knee to keep them front hitting the water that sat in the square enclosure beneath him, which meant the drain that was in the center of the enclosed tub-like

CM Books, LLC

square was closed. Sweat poured down Stone's face, and I didn't know if it was from him struggling to keep his legs bent or the fact that the battery cables were hooked to the chains that enclosed his wrists or the fact that maybe he didn't like snakes, especially the one Freak currently held in his hands.

"Mind if I sit in on the party, brothers?" I asked as I grabbed the chair against the wall, moved it in front of where Stone was hanging and sat down.

"Have at it, Moose. I was just about ready to let Jasmine show Stone some love," Freak said as he walked closer to Stone with the Boa wrapped around his neck and arms. When he started unwrapping it from his body, the snake began to wrap herself around Stone's waist and started to make her way up his body. I had to give it to Stone, he wasn't screaming even if he had lost control of his bladder.

"Stone, you can stop this anytime if you give us the information we want. Let's start with something easy like— who's the snitch that's left the club? Don't think of it as throwing someone under the bus because hey, we know someone has been giving you info; it's the only reason you were able to stay hidden from us for so long." I waited while he watched the snake work its way up his chest. When she reached his left shoulder and then slithered behind him to stretch across to the other shoulder, not only adding more weight to his already straining body but circling him until most of its body was wrapped around his neck and chest. I saw the panic in his eyes as they cut to me, but I wasn't sure it was enough for him to give over any information. Yet.

CM Books, LLC

"Fuck you and Haven. You think this shit is going to break me? There is nothing you can do to me that would be worse than what happens if I talk so go for it." I shook my head at his words, 'cause he was going to break, he just needed the ante upped.

"Oh, you mean Kosnoff. Think he is going to waste resources to come here to help you out? Jacks already said you didn't have anything to offer Kosnoff and that's why he stopped using you to run his drugs and cut you off. Oh, he kept you on the payroll while you were trying to regroup to try again to take over Haven, but you didn't count on someone else's initiative in stepping up and filling your spot, did you?" Without answering me, I knew I had Stone right where I wanted him. Between him and Jacks and their issues with trust, they were going to take the damn fun out of watching them break.

"You don't know dick. You think I don't know what you're trying to do? The whole lot of you think you are smarter than everyone else. Jacks only knows what I tell him and nothing more, so if you have Kosnoff info it came from someplace else because all that dumbshit knows is the man's name." Stone's breathing came harder the more he talked. Jasmine was putting her own pressure on him as she tightened against him.

"Having a little trouble breathing there? Every breath you take talking, Jasmine squeezes a little tighter, huh?" I watched as Stone tried to slow his breathing as the Boa tightened more on his chest. I glanced over at Freak who was watching closely, he knew when it would be time to unwrap his pet before she smothered Stone to death. Shock stood by waiting for his opportunity. He wouldn't turn the battery charger on as long as the snake was attached, Freak would never forgive him if Jasmine were harmed.

"You're not gonna kill me, you need me. You think Kosnoff didn't do his own checking? He knows about all of you, your families, your women." Stone sneered the last part. That told me he not only knew about Katie being Paul's daughter, he knew about her and I. Not good, but I would have to wait to handle that later.

"Ah, Stone, when did you lose your faith in us to get a job done. Isn't that why you took off? I'll tell you the same as I told Jacks, Kosnoff won't let loose ends dangle long." Stone started to cough and Freak moved in, and with Shock's help, they began to unwrap Jasmine from his body. Once he was freed from the snake's grasp, he took several deep breaths, but I noticed his legs trembled, and they had dropped almost to the water. It was time to push him harder.

"You don't know who you are messing with. Do you think I'm scared of what you can do to me?" Stone continued to talk and catch his breath at the same time. I waited and when his coughing eased, he went on. "Get on with it or take me back to my cell."

Stone no sooner got the words out that his feet hit the water, and Shock hit the switch on the battery. Stone screamed as the current shot through his body. Shock hit the switch again and the battery shut off.

"You're not in charge here, asshole," Shock warned.

"You know, I'm tired of this already. Never had much patience. So, Stone, when you are ready to talk, let Shock and Freak know. I'll be back when you have something to say." I stood and placed the chair back against the wall as Stone watched my every move. As I walked to the door, I reached in my pocket for the key. With the key in my hand, I turned to my brothers and nodded. "Do your thing and let me know when he's ready," I said and placed the key in the lock as Freak took the cover off a blacked-out box sitting on the table. I paused and watched as he reached in and pulled out his next surprise, his pet rattler. I inwardly shivered. Hell, if that didn't get the man to talk, we were going to have to do the old fashion way, beat him to an inch of his life.

"Sure you don't want to stick around and watch, Moose?" Freak asked as he held the snake in his hands. His hands and arms were covered in thick rubber gloves that reached well past his elbows.

"Nah, just make sure the anti-venom is close. Don't want him dying quite yet." I opened the door and walked out without a second glance at Stone. He'd learn real quick that he wasn't the only one who could play hardball.

I let the door shut behind me, and when it clicked, the sound of Stone's cries of pain were shut with it. I tested to make sure it locked and headed down the hall. I figured by the time I got back upstairs and talked with the others to see if anything else was found out, Stone would be more than ready to talk when I got back.

CM Books, LLC

# Chapter Five

## Katie

The brokerage offices of Stevens and Harris were on the top floor of the twenty-story high-rise. I stepped out of the elevator and walked up to the reception desk. My shift last night had been uneventful, which I was grateful, because after the chat with my dad yesterday, my mind hadn't been focused on work.

"Ms. Stevens, so nice to see you but your father isn't in," Carla said. She'd worked for the firm for as long as I could remember. "Oh shoot, I mean Dr. Stevens."

"Don't worry about it, Carla, it isn't a big deal. But is Mr. Harris in? I wanted to speak to him." She turned toward her computer and typed, then turned back to me.

"Mr. Harris is in but let me ring Brenda, his secretary, and see if he has time to see you." She picked up the phone and punched in Brenda's extension.

"I appreciate it, Carla," I said and waited while she spoke to Brenda and then sat the receiver down.

"Go on back, Dr. Stevens. Mr. Harris is free and will see you." I thanked Carla and headed down the hallway when I rounded the corner, Brenda's desk sat to the right in front of double wooden doors that were closed but led into Louis Harris's office.

"Hi, Dr. Stevens. Mr. Harris is on the phone, but if you take a seat, he'll see you when he's finished."

"Thanks," I said and sat in one of the leather chairs against the wall. Ten minutes couldn't have passed before Mr. Harris's voice come through Brenda's intercom to say he would see me now.

Brenda rose and went to the double doors, grabbed one handle, and opened the door. She stepped to the side to allow me to enter. Louis Harris came around his desk and hugged me. He was as tall as his son was when I'd last seen Linc and their similarities in looks were uncanny. Louis had the same dark hair with the exception of the gray that made an appearance at his temples, but the green eyes were the same shade he shared with his son. When I looked at Louis, I imagined that would be what Linc would look like when he reached his father's age.

"Katie-bug, you look great," he said, then held me at arm's length and looked me over. "I have a feeling I know why you are here. I'm sorry about all this, honey." I hadn't seen Mr. Harris for months. Not only had I lost Linc, but it had also felt like I'd lost a second family because I had spent so much time at their house.

"Mr. Harris, you have nothing to be sorry for. My dad brought all this on himself. I came to see you because I want to know the truth. I don't believe all he told me yesterday. How much trouble is my dad really in?" He led me to the chair in front of his desk and then took his own seat.

"I'm waiting for the auditing team's assessment to see how bad, and then the SEC will get involved. After speaking to my attorney, he made a discreet call to the DA, they went to law school together. Anyway, as soon as Kosnoff was mentioned, they knew exactly who he was, and none of it's good. The Feds have been after him for years, they can't get enough information on him to charge him with anything substantial. The man is into a lot of stuff, though. They even had one of their own go undercover to try to infiltrate Kosnoff's ranks, but they fingered him in less than a week, and the Feds damn near didn't get the agent out in time. Anyway, my attorney was told that Paul might be able to work out a plea for a lesser sentence if he turns evidence over against Kosnoff, but they couldn't guarantee it. That would have to come from the Feds, and it would depend on what and how much information Paul has to give them. But, Katie, please watch out if your dad does go that route, Kosnoff could come after you, your mother, or anyone who would give him the upper hand to keep your father quiet." We talked about everything Louis had found out so far, and I told him what I knew, and that the info had come from my father.

"I'll be careful, Mr. Harris, but I am a doctor, it's not like I can go into hiding. And even if I could, I'm not sure I would."

"I'd forgotten how stubborn you are. I used to tell Dana that I didn't know who was worse, you or Linc." Even though he smiled at me, it didn't reach his eyes. They seemed to reflect sadness or maybe disappointment.

"I can't answer that considering I haven't seen him in years. Sounds like he is where he needs to be. That he finally found what he was looking for. I'm glad." I stood and so did Louis.

"Yes, he has. However, I don't think he has everything to make his life complete." I knew where he was going and I refused to go there, so I walked toward the door. Since my dad first mentioned Linc's name, he'd been on my mind and I wasn't quite sure if I liked it.

"I would appreciate it if you would keep me posted on the audit or anything else you find out that involves my dad. I hate to say it, but I don't think he'll keep me up-to-date. I do know if he does have to serve time in jail, my mother will be the one to suffer more than him." I opened the door and stepped out of the office.

"I will, honey. Katie, your mom will be taken care of, no matter what happens to Paul." Louis stepped out of his office behind me.

"Yes, even if I have to do it myself, but I wasn't talking financially, her physical being is what worries me the most. Though her medication keeps her pretty balanced, I don't know if this will throw all that out of sync. We shall see, I suppose. Thanks for your time, Mr. Harris. I'm going home to get some sleep before my next shift at the hospital.

Hopefully, it won't take too long to get the ball rolling on this." I started to walk away when he called out my name.

"Katie?"

"Yes," I said as I stopped and turned back to face him.

"You know Linc will do everything he can to help your father."

"I don't doubt that since it will help his club, too."

"Yes, he would do anything for Haven."

I was willing to stick around to hear about Linc's loyalty to his club. I turned and started walking away once again.

"And you." My next step faltered at his final words. Once upon a time, I might have believed that.

The ringing woke me up, and I reached my hand out for my cell phone that sat on the nightstand by my bed. I didn't even look at the screen before I answered. "Dr. Stevens."

"Kosnoff's not happy with your dad. I think he's going to need an incentive to keep his mouth shut," the man said, then all that could be heard was a dial tone.

I sat up in bed and went to recent calls to see if a number showed but the only thing listed was Private Caller. The man's voice was deep and gravelly, one I couldn't recall ever hearing. I was sure I would have remembered it, he sounded like a smoker with a two pack a day habit.

The clock showed I had time to shower and get a bite to eat before my shift. It was a full moon, so it would be a long night because the crazies would be out in full force. I showered, dressed, and headed to the kitchen for something light to eat.

It didn't take long to heat the small microwave dinner and less time to eat it. I cleaned the few dishes in the sink, then walked down the hall and grabbed the bag with my gym clothes in it in case I felt like working out after I got off in the morning. Something I tried to do at least three times a week.

I hadn't pulled into the garage when I had come home that morning, so I walked out the front door of the condo I rented and headed for the driveway where my Mustang sat. The car had been my splurge when I was hired full-time at the hospital. It was fully loaded and the car was my baby.

The subdivision I lived in consisted of nothing but condos: two together, connected by the garages placed in the middle with the living space on each side. They were two bedrooms, two baths, and the layout in each was exactly the same. I rented mine as soon as I pulled my first paycheck. The area was nice, clean, and the rent was reasonable, which meant most living in the subdivision were single or families just starting out.

I disengaged the alarm to the car and inserted my key just as I heard the motorcycle approaching and the garage door next door starting to rise. I opened my car door, then turned to watch as my new neighbor pulled up on a black Harley. I loved motorcycles, but I hadn't ridden on one since Linc had taken me for rides on the one he had gotten for his high school graduation. The one we had been riding the night he told me he was leaving. I shook my head to clear that train of thought because I didn't need to go there before work. Instead, I smiled as I watched my neighbor dismount and pull the helmet off her head and walk toward me, the sun shining off her red hair that she had pulled back in a braided ponytail.

"Hey, Katie, going to work?" Charlie asked when she stopped in front of me.

"Yeah, last shift, then four whole days off. I'm so ready."

"I know what you mean, my time off has gone by fast. I start my new job in a week. I finally got everything organized and put away. Moving sucks." Charlie looked up and down the street and then back at me.

"What do you do? I never asked you last week when you moved in." I'd only talked with her shortly one day when I ran into her as the moving company was unloading in front of our place.

"Oh, I'm a bounty hunter." My jaw dropped when I looked at the woman, and she laughed.

"Wow, that would have been the last job I would have placed you doing." I laughed with her.

"I get that look all the time when I tell people what I do. But if you think about it, I would be the last person that a runner would think was after them. I'm able to get close to them without them even suspecting they've been caught." When she smiled, her whole face lit up, and her green eyes sparkled.

CM Books, LLC

I looked down at my watch, "Ugh, I need to leave to get to the hospital on time. We are going to have to get together while I'm off. I would love to hear more about your work." Charlie had to be close to my age, and she seemed genuine and nice, and I liked her.

"That sounds great. Let's get together tomorrow night. I bought a new grill, we could cook out and drink, then you can tell me where all the hot men hang out around here." I laughed and turned and got in my car.

"You're on, well except for where the hot guys hang out because I haven't a clue."

"I find that hard to believe. See you tomorrow. Is six good? Then you can tell me how a woman that looks like you, doesn't know where the men are."

"That works, see you then." We said goodbye, and I closed my door as she turned and headed back to her place.

Charlie would be shocked when I told her I hadn't had a steady boyfriend since I was sixteen. I tried to date a couple of times in college but had given up when both men couldn't stand up against Linc. Damn it all to hell, I said I wasn't going to think about him. I reached out, turned the music up loud, and pushed down on the gas pedal, it was enough to push Linc right out my head.

CM Books, LLC

# Chapter Six

## Moose

We sat around the table in the Prez's office to discuss anything new that had been found out.

"You first, Moose. How is Stone holding up?" Prez asked and leaned back in the chair.

"He hasn't broken yet, but when we are done, I will go back down. Don't think it's going to take too much longer. Stone acts tough, which plays to our advantage because he likes to talk about how smart and tough he is. The read I got on him so far is that he is scared of Kosnoff for one. Two, Jacks knows a lot, maybe not everything, but Stone tried too hard to play Jacks off as an idiot who only knows what Stone tells him."

"What makes you think Jacks knows more than that," Hawk interrupted me and asked.

"He was Sergeant of Arms for Haven long before me, and you can't do this job without some ability to read people. I'll bet Jacks knows everything and if he was present when

71

things were getting discussed, well, he could know more than Stone. People tend not to pay attention to the muscle in the room. And if that is how Jacks portrayed himself around Kosnoff and his people, they could have slipped up and said something in front of him. So if Stone doesn't start talking, we will start on Jacks, he won't break per se, but if he feels Stone is pushing him under the bus, he'll spill. Self-preservation mode will kick in."

"How do you know that?" Keg asked.

"Loyalty to Stone is the only thing that is keeping Jacks quiet. As soon as Stone breaks that loyalty, then he won't feel obligated to help Stone. I was with Jacks before I went into the room with Stone, and the doubt is there. He will wait and see how Stone acts when we put him back in the cell beside him. Give them a few minutes together, alone, then take Jacks out. If Stone holds out this first go around, Jacks could go either way—continue to follow Stone or spill what he knows hoping we will cut him some slack."

"Brother, you do realize you are kinda scary with that shit. Makes me want to start watching what I say around you," Crank said, and I chuckled.

"No shit. Hope you don't have profiles wrote up on each of us," Pinch added.

"I don't think they make file folders that extend wide enough to hold any of your profiles," I said, then laughed when the others gave me the finger.

"Alright, let's move on. Tram, what do you have for us?" Wild Bill asked. Tram's specialty dealt with anything to do with electronics, and if a computer system was hackable,

72

he was in. I couldn't count how many times that particular skill came in handy when a terrorist held a phone in his hand ready to blow something up, and Tram would find where the signal was bouncing off towers, jam it, rendering the device useless.

"I won't go into too much detail. I'll just cover where and what I found. The SEC is already looking into Paul Stevens. From what I came across, they've been at it for about two months. I'm thinking the Feds are the ones to clue them in because when I jumped over, they have been busy looking at Kosnoff for approximately six months. I figure they followed the money trail back to Stevens and Harris Brokerage, then called the SEC in on Paul. The SEC has enough to take down Paul, but they haven't and it made me curious, so I dug deeper and found out why. There seems to have been money of substantial amounts generated from Taiwan, Japan, China, and several other Asian countries that bounced from several banks. It even went through a Swiss bank, stayed there for a few days, then bounced somewhere else before ending up in Kosnoff's shipping company's brokerage account to be spread out between different stocks. Some of it would transfer back from a quick buy and sell trade, and that would go directly into Kosnoff's personal account." Tram stopped and took a drink from the glass in front of him.

"How the hell is that not enough to nail Kosnoff on?" Pinch asked.

"Because every time the money bounced, the total changed. They would add together say two amounts, then

73

the next time it bounced somewhere the balance was different than the first transaction. They started out with like fifty accounts, and by the time they made the last bounce, it was one amount until it hit the brokerage firm where it was split again several times with different amounts each time."

"Did you find what the money from the other countries was paying for? Shipment costs, maybe?" Crank asked, then leaned back in his chair.

"Trafficking was what the FBI has listed." Before Tram could finish our prez interrupted.

"Guns, drugs...people? Which one?" the Prez asked.

"All of the above. One other thing surfaced, too. Moose, your dad had their company lawyer give him a list of attorney names that handled these types of cases."

"Did you get that digging through my dad's stuff?"

"No, the Feds had a note referring to it. They want Paul to flip on Kosnoff. The note also said that as of right now, Paul wasn't willing to do it. They have a flight watch, too. They think if he is pushed into a corner, he will either cut a deal with them or take off. That is pretty much all I got." Tram closed the file in front of him and leaned back in his chair.

"That was a lot, Tram. Nice job," Wild Bill said, then turned to face Pinch and Keg. "You and Pinch are up."

"Pinch and I went to the house, Prez, and you were right, there was still some boxes out in your storage shed that had been boxed up from Stone's trailer after he left. It was mostly pictures and whatnot shit you thought Carly might want of her mother's stuff. We were almost done going

74

through it all when Pinch came across a little notebook that was between some books. He started flipping the pages while I finished going through the box to look for anything else that might have gotten overlooked that day when it was getting packed, so I will let Pinch tell you what it contained." Keg nodded to Pinch when he finished.

As I sat and listened, I couldn't believe how much we had uncovered in half a day. It all wasn't making sense right now, but it would once I spread the information out in front of me and moved it around until the info pretty much told a story. It was almost like putting a puzzle together.

"It took me a little while to decipher what was in the notebook. There were numbers and letters in columns, and beside them were dates. We brought it back with us." Pinch set the notebook on the table and pushed it to Wild Bill. "You can see for yourself. Figured you want to lock that up, I scanned the whole thing into the computer. Gotta say I spent way too much time trying to figure it out until it hit me that it was Stone's and no way in hell did that dumbass have some elaborate coding system. So when that hit me, well, I did the basic. The numbers switch to alphabet letters, which spell out names, then the letters in the next column give you amounts when switched over. One section is showing deposits and withdrawals on an account. When I searched club accounts, it was to one that you had closed and transferred the money to another account after Stone left. The deposit went in and then on the next line a portion came out. That portion was listed into another ledger of sorts, and part was paid out every time to the same account, same amount, monthly. The account that part was going into wasn't an account of the club's, but it is the same bank where we do business. I called the bank, but Madison wasn't working today,and she didn't answer her cell, but I left a message for her to call me. She will look that up for us and tell us who is on that account. There was another set of columns in the back of the notebook that was the most interesting. It was money paid and deposited into yet another account. That was Stone's personal account because in the boxes we found an old statement with that number on it and it is with another bank. Give you guys each a guess where that bank account is." Pinch paused to see if any of us would play.

Cal Wetzel was given the name Pinch while prospecting for Haven after he told us the story of how he came back from his stint in the Army with almost all his pay. He'd only spent enough to live on because he wanted to save and be able to help his sister, Madison, with college. Penny Pincher was too long of a road name, so he became Pinch.

I grinned and answered, "I only need one. A bank in Canada."

"Damn, Moose, you are right. That is what we found today. Only need Madison to get us the other information," Pinch finished, and Crank was staring at him. "What?"

"You're seriously going to bring Mad into this. They find out she is giving out names and account numbers, she could lose her job." Pinch squinted his eyes at Crank while the rest of us sat back to watch. The two had joined Haven together, they'd been friends since middle school.

CM Books, LLC

"Madison isn't going to lose her job. She is over the accounts at the bank. Give me a little credit. And why are you so concerned about her anyway. Your ass better not be sniffin' around my sister, asshole. She is too young for you." Pinch crossed his arms over his chest.

"Young? We are only six years older than her." Crank chuckled.

"Just fucking stay away from her. I don't even want you to go to the bank and see her," Pinch said and turned back to the rest of us ending their conversation.

"Hawk, Crank, and I met with General Patel. He handed over the package for the next mission. We've got pics and individual statistics on each cell member known to be in the area. The only thing he told us was there are four men and one woman. When we get a chance, we will lay it out to get a better picture of what we'll be facing. You will be going to Boston this time, boys," Wild Bill said.

Groans came from each of us. Boston was hell to move around in on a good day, add the marathon traffic to the equation, and it was going to be damn near impossible. We'd do it but fuck it was going to suck.

"Let's plan to look through this stuff day after tomorrow." The Prez stood and we followed suit. And just as I stood my phone buzzed. I reached into my pocket to see who had texted and read the text.

I shoved the phone in my pocket and looked at the others. "That was dad. The audit is coming in tomorrow. He said he would come to us."

"Sounds good. If we are lucky, you can get us some more information from Jacks or Stone, and we will be one more step ahead of Kosnoff. Moose, with all we learned, if Paul cooperates with the Feds, Kosnoff could go after your girl to keep him quiet. If Paul doesn't cooperate, Kosnoff could still go after your girl anyway to send a message to him. Have you thought about that yet?"

"Yeah, I have. I'm working out a plan on that. But I need to get this over with Stone first. What I get from him or Jacks will let me know how it should be handled."

"Then get to it." Wild Bill slapped me on the shoulder.

I nodded, told my brothers I would see them in a few, and headed to the basement.

# Chapter Seven

## Moose

How the hell Freak and Shock could stand the smell in the room was beyond me. It made me wonder just how bad being a POW had been on them. It brought another level of respect for the older men.

When I walked back in after I had met with the others, it was to find Stone still hanging by his wrist but passed out. His chest was moving, which at least showed he was still breathing, but his breaths were a little labored. It seemed a person could get bit by a rattler several times in fact, and if the anti-venom was readily handy, survive.

Shock had recorded Stone's ramblings while I had been absent, he knew I would want to go over every word out of the asshole's mouth. He looked like death was knocking at his door, but other than faint burn marks on the bottom of his feet, where the current from the battery tried to escape his body, and the five or six sets of puncture wounds from the snake bites, he'd live. It would be with a

79

few scars from the bites, but he would continue to breathe as he lived out the rest of his life in prison. With his attitude, though, it would be a short life on the inside.

We unhooked Stone and took him back to his cell. That had been a couple of hours ago. We left him and Jacks alone just like we'd discussed earlier, and I'd spent that time listening to the recorder. The tape was proof that if enough pain were administered to a man, they'd tell you their life story. So needless to say, when the door opened, and I got a good look at Jacks' face as Freak and Stone led him in, it told me the plan had been effective and that Stone more or less talked in his weakened state.

"Just sit him in that extra chair. He can't get out of here, and I don't think we are going to have to strap him up and use your methods this time around." I watched Freak pull the chair to the center of the room and position it to face me.

"I want to know what the hell that rat bastard spouted off about," Jacks said as Shock pushed him down into the chair.

"Ah, now you want to talk?" I cocked a brow at him.

"You know the deal, Moose. My loyalty is with Stone, we joined Haven together under Wild Bill's dad. And did you really expect for me to talk when you brought us here, so you could turn around and kill us sooner?"

"Who gave you the idea we were going to kill ya?" I thought I knew, I just wanted him to verify it for me.

"We saw the news where you killed Jacob and Don, then burnt the bodies in that house fire." I wanted to smile,

CM Books, LLC

that had taken some doing. The General stepped in for us, and we ended up paying for the cadavers from the nearby college that were used. The house had been an old one that was on the controlled burn list for the local fire department. But the cost for the manpower and the bodies was worth it.

"Jacks, Spud, and Tater should be glad we didn't give them over to the Black Hawk MC. We did them one last service of being members of this club at one time. Only people to blame for their actions are themselves for being dumb enough to follow Stone in the first place.

"Now, you want to tell me why the hell you were down in Black Hawk territory? Don't say it was all for Carly either. You might feed that bullshit to someone else, but we know better."

Jacks stared blankly at me; his expression guarded. I imagined he was debating his chances once everything was revealed. Freak moved closer to the snakes' cages, and Jacks' eyes shifted to him. When he looked back at me; his expression had changed to reveal defeat.

"Stone planned to use Carly to get her dad to help us out with Wild Bill. He hadn't done his research, so he didn't know Wild Bill had been in the service with the leaders from Black Hawk. Stone was mad that Wild Bill hid Carly and Sami there because we were going to use them against him."

"Was that when Stone was going to let you and Creeper have a little fun with her before Kosnoff said he wanted her to be pure because she'd bring a bigger price?" I watched the shock form on his face.

81

"Goddamn, did that asshole tell you that? We didn't make any deal like that. Why would Creeper and I want some young girl with more of a boy's shape than a woman's? We didn't need her to have a good time, the bitch's mother was more than willing to take and give us what we wanted, the more, the merrier, too." I stopped him on that little rant because I knew it was a crock of shit.

"Don't call Carly a bitch, especially when you actually knew her; she was a teenager who lost her mother, though she had a father in Stone until he found out she wasn't really his and decided to make her pay for her mother's deception. And you and Creeper not interested? Jacks, the club cleaned out your places after you took off with Stone. We found it all, the pics, the videos you had purchased and hidden behind the others on your TV stand. We even found a couple of emails and chats with young girls on your computer. Thank God, those little girls' families had taught them right. You closed your account, even did a basic scrub on the hard drive, that is the only reason they hadn't busted you for it, they couldn't find you when the parents turned you two into the police, but nothing ever really goes away if you know where to look for it. Made me want to vomit when we brought up the video you had sent of you jacking off and asking that girl to take her shirt off. You and Creeper are two sick and perverted individuals. What'd you do with those videos? Watch them with Creeper and beat your meat while little girls took their clothes off on the screen?" Jacks' eyes flashed, and I knew I'd pushed the right buttons with him.

CM Books, LLC

He was cut from the same cloth as Stone and trying to cover for his own self.

"You bastard," Jacks yelled as he went to lunge at me from his chair. It didn't work out for him since Shock and Freak stood on each side of him. When Shock hit him with the charge from the battery cables, Jacks fell back onto the chair.

"When you catch your breath and your ears stop ringing, start fucking talking because if you don't, Freak here is going to give you a little dose of what Stone dealt with." Jacks' eyes followed Freak as he pulled on his gloves and lifted the lid off the rattler's cage. When Freak's hand reached in, Jacks started talking. At one point, I pulled out my phone and texted Wild Bill so he could line a few things up.

Jacks answered every question I asked and then some. By the time we were finished, I could have killed him and Stone and never blinked an eye. When we were done, the three of us walked Jacks back to his cell next to Stone's.

"What did you tell them, Jacks?" Stone asked as I shut the cell door. Jacks laid on his cot and rolled over, giving his back to Stone. "I'm going to have you killed, and it's going to be a nice slow death!" Stone shouted at me after Jacks ignored him.

I laughed, and so did Shock and Freak who stood by the open door.

"Yeah, I'm scared, Stone," I said and started toward the door.

CM Books, LLC

"Kosnoff will do it, too. What you did to me will be nothing compared to what he will do to you!"

"He is going to be too busy to worry about any of us, thanks to the two of you."

Stone pushed up off his cot and stood. "What are you talking about? You've got nothing. I didn't say shit." Stone leaned against the bars. I reached into my pocket and took out the small recorder and pushed play. Stone's whole demeanor changed when his voice was heard as it began playing. "You can't prove any of that!"

"Ah, but I don't have to."

Stone and Freak moved apart, and I walked out with them on my heels. I heard the door close and lock, but kept walking until I was out in the common room before I turned around.

"Are they gettin' picked up in the morning?" Shock asked.

"Sometime tomorrow," I answered and smiled at the two men. I knew what was bothering him. "They'll be out of your way tomorrow. Go have a cold beer before you hit the sheets."

"What about the other issue?" Freak asked.

"Ah, when we are done, they won't be our problem." I headed for the stairs that led up to the main clubhouse floor. I heard two doors shut as I started up the stairs.

I knew when I reached the first floor that the others would be there, Wild Bill had called Church after I had texted him.

84

When I reached his office, I knocked and waited. The day had already been long and was looking to get longer.

CM Books, LLC

CM Books, LLC

# Chapter Eight

## Moose

"Open!" Wild Bill yelled, and I opened the door and walked into his office. The others were already seated, waiting. After I had taken my place, Keg slapped me on the back.

"You called that shit right, again," he said, then handed me six one hundred dollar bills. I looked over at the Prez.

"What? Did you think I wasn't going to go in on the bet?" The others chuckled at the Prez's words.

"I didn't take you as a man who likes throwing away money," I said and pulled my wallet out to place the money in it.

"I don't. But paying you on how long it would take to get those fuckers talking, was well worth it. They become the Feds' issue tomorrow, and Haven will be one step closer to being on track. Haven't been able to say that for several years. It feels damn good."

87

"You got that right," Hawk agreed, and so did the others.

"As much as I enjoy taking your money, were you able to get ahold of Latch?" I asked Keg.

"Yeah, he headed out with Taylor and Sparks after I called him. He checked in after they got to the hospital, Kathryn was still there. She doesn't..." he looked at his watch, "get off for another four hours. They'll hang there, and then they will take shifts at her place when she goes home. Latch caught one of the orderlies on a smoke break and started a conversation with him. He found out she is off for a few days when she finishes her shift today. That will make shit a lot easier," Keg finished, and I nodded.

"Okay, let's start Church and see where we are at. Hit us, Moose, with what all you've learned. I gotta ask, though, why don't you just let us listen to the recording?" Prez asked.

It would have been much easier, but the blowback on some of the news was going to hit hard and close to home like it had done for me when I first heard it.

"I want to start with the stuff dealing with Kosnoff and Stone's involvement with him first because when I get to the part about Haven, tempers are going to flare." The Prez and the others sat up straighter in their chairs with all eyes on me.

"Fair enough. No one interrupts him. Save any questions for after Moose is done," the Prez said, then crossed his arms. "Begin."

I nodded in reply, then jumped right in. "Stone got mixed up with Kosnoff when he came across a post that

CM Books, LLC

most people would have overlooked because it talked about buying and selling young chicks, it had everything that made the site look as though they were dealing in poultry when actually it dealt with the selling of young girls. Stone, Jacks, and Creeper liked to dabble with the young and trust me that is putting it mildly. Stone met with a man and they worked out a deal on Stone and his boys getting the use of a few young girls for free if they would transport and sell drugs and guns for them. The man he made a deal with worked for Kosnoff.

"After a while, Stone saw the amount of drugs and the cash coming in for them and started skimming both. You don't get to where Kosnoff is by being stupid, and it didn't take him long to figure it out. To keep from being killed, Stone cut a deal, not only would they continue what they were doing for Kosnoff already, they stepped it up a level and started supplying young girls for the trafficking part of Kosnoff's operation. Since Stone and the boys were doing such a good job, Kosnoff promised to help him take over Haven, so there was nothing or no one to step in their way.

"Paul Stevens, Kathryn's dad, pretty much ended up in the same circumstance as Stone when he used bad judgment in borrowing Kosnoff's money to try to make himself more. Kosnoff kept Paul in line by threatening his family but what he didn't tell Paul was they had no intention of harming his wife, only Kathryn. That is why I texted you and then wanted some men on her. I also have an idea that might push Paul enough to be a willing participant in taking Kosnoff down. Something the Feds have been trying to do but can't get near the man. It doesn't help that they never knew what he looked like before, they only had his name and that he is Russian, wealthy, and loved in the shipping industry.

"They at least know what he looks like now, though, since I texted my dad and had him dig in his pictures and find the one with Kosnoff in it and had my dad forward it to the Feds. The man has never been married, but he has had plenty of women, women no one can locate after he is done with them. And while they were with him, they tended not to want to bite the hand that was feeding them so they wouldn't give any information on him." I stopped and took a drink out of the coke can that was sitting on the table when I came in. My brothers must have known I would need the caffeine boost and beer was out of the question, at least while attending to business.

"Goddamn, that shit could be a movie or at the very least a book. What happened that made Stone run, instead of staying and using Kosnoff's help in taking over?" Hawk asked.

"Several things led to it. Carly moving in with the Prez was one. Stone, Jacks, and Creeper were going to sell her off to Kosnoff for trafficking." The look on Keg's and Wild Bill's faces were ones of murder. I had already had that moment when Jacks had said it downstairs. "Add to that, he had been selling drugs within the club. The ready supply that was available to Carly's mom started to cost him, and finally, when Wild Bill started to question and get rid of some of the members who had lost their way due to the drugs, Stone's backing was diminishing, which gave someone else the opportunity to step in. The final thing that sent him on the run was he started skimming again, and it wasn't just from Haven. Some of that in the notebook Pinch went through was Kosnoff's money. I'm going to take it that Madison hasn't gotten back to you on that account, has she?" I asked, and Pinch shook his head no.

"No need for her to comprise her job. The money was going into that account for a reason. And that is the reason for our latest couple of issues in the club. Plus, I have a gut feeling it is more than just dealing with Stone and Jacks. We have to let that one lay for just a little while longer because we don't want Kosnoff to take off to Russia before the Feds have everything they need to take him down and charge him. They want him for it all. It's the best chance they're going to get at the man."

"How are they expecting to get him on the trafficking? Only hope they are going to have is with Stone and Jacks, and that is if they know where and how Kosnoff's people are doing it," Crank interrupted.

"That is why you had me call the General, so he could push the Feds to look into the case they are working on against Paul?" I nodded in agreement with Prez, and then he yelled, "Sonofabitch, those fake e-trade accounts Mr. Stevens set up. Fuckers weren't Kosnoff's fake accounts, they were trafficking payments from the damn buyers of the girls he was selling."

My lips twitched; I would have bet money on one of them figuring that out when I laid everything out for them.

91

"Did you get that from Stone or Jacks, or did you figure it out? 'Cause I gotta say if you figured that out, Moose, you are one scary and smart motherfucker," Tram said and coming from him that was a helluva a compliment.

"He uses that woo-woo thinking while we are out on the job. How the fuck do you think he always figures out where the terrorist assholes are holding up?" Keg said and smacked Tram on the back.

"Prez is correct. Stone and Jacks both mentioned some accounts that were set up for the buyers to funnel money, and I knew Paul had set the fake accounts up, it wasn't a far reach. We should know soon enough on those. The trafficking, they used the Peace Arch Crossing and knew the times the guard they had on payroll would be working. Which by the way, they're probably being picked up now for questioning and that is going to piss Kosnoff off when he finds out. Anyway, they would take them up to Vancouver, cross into Alaska and head to the Bering Sea.

"If you recall, a while back the news said a Chinese ship was spotted close by, well, it was Kosnoff's buyer picking up. Sometimes his own ships would if they were making the journey back to Vladivostok because it would have been easy to do drops or arrange a pick up for them since Tokyo, Japan; Beijing, China; and Korea, all set close to the Sea of Japan and the North Pacific. The man has greased so many hands that when they do take him down, a lot of jobs are going to open after everyone goes down who is on the man's payroll.

"Not that I give a shit, because Kosnoff is the Feds problem; at least now I know Kathryn will be safe." I took another drink to prepare for the next bit of information I had to share. I could tell Wild Bill was getting impatient because his leg bounced under the table and his fingers tapped on the top.

"Alright, is that it with the club? Other than waiting to handle the last two issues," Wild Bill asked.

"No, just a couple more things. Some you know already from the shit that went down with Carly and the Black Hawk MC. Stone admitted to killing Speed's dad and their mom by fixing the needle that caused her overdose, and then he dumped her body in an alley by a dumpster. That happened after he found out Carly wasn't his kid and her mom had threatened to leave and take her to Cutter, her and Speed's dad.

"The Haven VP from before Stone was Ratchet, right?" I looked at Wild Bill.

"Yeah, he and my dad had been best friends. They grew up together in the club." Wild Bill's brow furrowed, and I knew when it hit him. "Are you telling me that fucker was responsible for Ratchet's death, too?" He pushed his chair back, stood, and slammed his hands down on the table.

"Yes, Stone and Jacks. Stone promised Jacks he would talk your dad into bringing him into the leadership."

"Goddamn, I should go down and kill that motherfucker now." Wild Bill walked back and forth across the office floor. We sat and watched until he walked up and stood in front of me. "Stone and Jacks were with my dad when he was shot. They told me he died on the spot and they couldn't bring him back because the damn deal they were doing went bad and they had to get out quick. I never questioned them about leaving his body behind. I had his body sent from the morgue to the mortuary. That was after the cops notified me of his death and then they told me that he was shot in an open field and the only evidence that others were there was the tire tracks left behind." As I looked over at Keg when Wild Bill put his hand on Keg's shoulder, Keg didn't look up. He sat there with his head bowed.

It was quiet in the office while we let the two men take a few minutes to grieve again for the loss of their family member. As I watched them, I tried to imagine what I would do if my dad had been killed and I had the man responsible in arm's reach. It was too late now, but I should've waited to tell them after the Feds picked Stone and Jacks up.

We'd been in Church for so long that the sun was up and shining through the blinds. I pulled my phone out of my pocket to check the time, and it buzzed just as someone knocked on the door. I read the text from Latch letting me know that Kathryn was gathering her stuff to leave, and he would be the one to watch her at home for the first shift instead of Taylor. I texted Latch back to let him know I would be at my house if he needed me and when I looked back up, Roach stepped in the office.

"Feds are pulling around the back, Prez," Roach said, then looked at the rest of us and lifted his chin.

"How the hell do you know they are Feds?" Wild Bill asked.

"I might be old, but my damn eyes work."

I shook my head. Roach was the next oldest member in the Haven behind Shock and Freak.

"Alright, old man, we were just finishing up. Let them in the basement and I'll meet them down there."

"You got it, Prez." Roach turned and walked out, and I would have sworn I heard him mumbling about Wild Bill's dad rolling over in his grave with Haven cooperating with the Feds.

Wild Bill turned back to us. "Moose, we still meeting your dad this afternoon?"

"No need now. He is going to work on Paul to try to get him to cooperate with the Feds and the SEC. Paul's going to lose his license, there's no getting around it. They've got an attorney that is supposed to come by tomorrow, and they are hoping he will be able to keep Paul out of jail. We'll see."

"Okay, why don't you go home, get some rest. I'll handle the turnover of the two downstairs. Keg, Hawk, you both can help the Feds get them loaded. The rest of you get out of here, too. I'm going home when I am done. Call me and keep me posted on our last issue. My granddaughter's birthday party is next weekend, I want that handled before Keg and I head to Black Hawk."

Ally, Wild Bill's granddaughter was a pistol and had the man wrapped around her finger. No long after Sami and Carly were sent to Shades Valley, Sami got pregnant but

95

wouldn't tell her dad and brother who the father was. No matter how much the Prez badgered her. Ally was born, and we all wondered if we would ever find out who fathered the little girl. It was answered when Speed, a member of the Black Hawk MC, came home from the military four years later to take his father's place as enforcer in the club. Sami had met Speed when he was home on leave when his dad, Cutter, had been killed in a motorcycle accident. Which now we all knew was because of Stone. He had no clue his one night with Sami resulted in Ally until his return and his accidental run-in with the little girl. And since she looked just like him, there was no denying he was her dad.

"The clubs got a few presents for you to take Ally. We'll make sure to get them to your house before the two of you leave," I said and stood.

"Yeah, 'cause she won't receive enough stuff already. Prez wouldn't let me get a Haven vest made for her," Keg said.

"Because you only wanted to do it to cause trouble," Wild Bill said and slapped Keg on the back.

"Me? Never," Keg said, and the rest of us laughed.

"Let's save the discussion on your loss of memory with the shit you've done over the years for another time. I want this club shit handled and done," Wild Bill said and waited for no reply as he headed to the door.

We followed him out of the office and when we reached the main room, Crank, Tram, and I headed out the front door to get on our bikes while the others headed in the opposite direction.

CM Books, LLC

It felt good when the fresh air and sun hit my face. And it felt even better when I walked into my house. I showered to wash away the stench of the hours I'd spent dealing with Stone and Jacks, but they weren't Haven's problem any longer.

I dropped in my bed and closed my eyes and brought up Kathryn's face. First thing on my list was done, now my woman needed to be claimed. I smiled when I thought of how she was going to act, but it didn't matter, in the end, she'd be exactly where she was meant to be—with me.

97

CM Books, LLC

# Chapter Nine

## Katie

The smoke from Charlie's grill billowed in the air as I stepped out my back door. I debated locking it, but the neighborhood was a decent one, and I would only be next door. When I turned the corner of our garages' wall, Charlie stood in front of the grill flipping steaks as she danced in place to the music that was probably coming out of the iPod earpieces she wore.

"Charlie!" I yelled her name so as not to scare the crap out of her by walking up behind her. She looked over her shoulder and smiled, then reached up and pulled the buds out of her ears.

"Hey, girl. I was going to get these done and come over and knock. I thought maybe you were still sleeping from your shift last night." She grabbed the pan beside the grill and pulled the steaks off.

"No, I only slept for a few hours. I want to be able to go to bed tonight. When I have days off after coming off the night shift, it's the only way to get back to normal hours. If not, I'd want to stay up all night and sleep all day."

"I know that feeling. When I'm staking out a place for a jumper, I could be there for hours if not the whole day and night," Charlie said as she walked in her place and I followed with the salad I had made to go with dinner.

"I hope this doesn't offend you, it is hard to believe you can take a man down." I chuckled, and so did she.

"That, hon, is why I can. Most of them don't expect it because when they look at me, they focus on me being a woman first and before they figure out that I have the skill, it's too late." We placed everything on her kitchen table and sat down to eat. "Oh, I forgot to grab the drinks." Charlie stood back up and went to her fridge when she held up the beers, I nodded. I didn't have to worry about getting up in the morning, and I wasn't even on call either, so I was going to enjoy myself.

"Yesterday, you mentioned you moved here for a job. I can't imagine moving across the country by myself even for that," I said.

"I didn't just do it for the job. My grandfather was last known to live here. I wanted to try to find him. I've never met him. For all I know he might not be alive." She picked up her silverware and started to eat, and I followed suit.

"How did you find out about the job? Can't say I have ever seen an ad for a bounty hunter listed under the 'Help Wanted' section of the paper."

"I met two of the Matherson brothers when we crossed paths on a case, seemed we were searching for the

CM Books, LLC

same person. They ended up with the capture because when I got to where the guy was supposed to be, they were chasing him down the block as I pulled up. At the curb, I waited for the guy to reach me and I threw the door open on my truck. The guy went down, and they were on him before he stood back up. They cut me in on their take and offered me a job. Hadn't really thought about moving but when they told me their business was located in Washington state, I took the opportunity since I knew it was the state my grandfather lived in. And here I am," Charlie finished and we continued to eat in silence. When we were done, I helped her clean up the small number of dishes there were, and then we grabbed another beer each and took our two-person party out on the patio. It was nice to sit back and relax with someone else: no drama, no men, no work.

"So tell me, why don't you have a man instead of having to sit here with me?" Charlie tipped her beer and raised her brow at me.

"What makes you think I don't have a man?"

"Oh, hon, really? Your looks, you're a doctor, but mainly it is because I live next door and since I moved in, I haven't seen one guy come or go from your place. If you had a steady that so would not be the case," she said and laughed when I just looked at her.

"Uh… I could say the same about you, too."

"Touché. But in my defense, I've just moved here."

"You work in a male dominant field, come on, it shouldn't be too hard to scrape up a man."

CM Books, LLC

"True, but I want to be taken seriously at this job so mixing pleasure with it, not possible. I will say if I ever did, girl, those brothers would be prime candidates for fraternizing with. Mmmm... Mmmm. When I met Josh and Jake on that job, damn, I thought that gene pool got it right, two men who looked like they did, well, there couldn't be anymore. Didn't even think of it when they said they had two more brothers that were in the business with them. Flew out to meet everyone and discuss working with them and I gotta admit, those men ooze sex. No mistaken they are brothers either. They are tall, dark, and with their smoky gray eyes, they pull a look off that should be illegal. I imagine they have no problem with women dropping panties around them wherever they go. Hell, I wanted to drop mine." She laughed and then looked at me and smiled.

"What?" I asked.

"Now *you* don't work for them."

"No, no, no. I think I will keep my panties on." I laughed then. I knew all about men who looked like Charlie's description of the Matherson brothers. At least one and if I closed my eyes I could picture him, which I'd done the last couple days to the point that after I thought of him, I wondered how much he'd changed since I'd seen him last. That was when *Mr. Big* was taken out of his handy case and used until I was breathless but still unsatisfied.

Linc would have filled out more and have a man's build instead of the young man he'd been when he left. I needed to push that thought away because it might be

CM Books, LLC

considered rude to orgasm on Charlie's patio, especially since I didn't know her that well.

"Damn, what put that look on your face? Or should I ask, who? I expected you to moan any second." She took a drink of her beer and watched me as I tried to get my system under control.

"Just my past," I said and took my own drink to cool off a little.

"Hon, people don't usually have that expression when they look back on their past. Not unless that was some past. Know what I'm saying?"

"Yeah, but the fact it is part of my past, hadn't been my choice, it was his. So I have to respect that, right?"

"Fuck no. Does he live close? 'Cause if he does, you should turn that frown you're wearing now into a smile. Better yet, you should be letting *him* do it for you."

I couldn't help but laugh. Charlie was too funny, and I enjoyed her company a lot.

"I know he lives around here, just not where. Avoidance is a wonderful tool."

"My ass would find out real quick like. Men who can put that look on a woman's face don't stay single too long. Those are the type of men that women will claw another's eyes out to be owned by them. In the physical sense. I mean not own as in 'do as I say' outside the bedroom."

I couldn't help but laugh. The woman was a riot. "Charlie, this is great. It's been forever since I've felt this relaxed and more like the old me. The woman who reached for what she wanted and didn't care what people thought.

CM Books, LLC

So, we are going to have to do this again. Next time, my place."

"Yeah, we are. And stick with me, I help you get the old you back. How about another beer?" Charlie asked.

"Sounds good." She got up, went inside, and when she came back, it was with two beers each. "Saving another trip in?"

"Yeah, and I have plenty more where that came so drink up. I say let's get drunk, it'll make the stories we tell a lot more interesting." Charlie chuckled, and I shook my head.

We sat and talked about our jobs. Charlie told me about some of her most interesting experiences since she had become a bounty hunter. I'd never laughed so hard. But when she talked about the first time she rode on the back of a bike, I choked on my beer and damn near fell out of the chair.

"Hold up. Did you just call me a dumbass?" Charlie asked, and I straightened in my chair.

"No, I was too busy laughing. What the heck are you talking about?" I asked.

"Damn, I'm tipsy already. I closed my eyes for a minute and thought I heard a soft thud. I figured you might have fallen out of the chair and was going to look, but before I opened my eyes I could have sworn you called me a dumbass. I haven't drank in a while and this beer must be hitting me hard. I'm going to feel like shit in the morning."

"Well, probably. You've drank two for every one I've had." I chuckled, and she flipped me off. I was feeling

CM Books, LLC

lightheaded myself but probably nowhere near as bad off as Charlie. "Let's go in and have some of that cake I made today and forgot to bring over earlier. It might soak up some of the alcohol in your system."

"You did? Hell, when did you go over to your place and get that?"

"After we finished the first six-pack. Which for you was about a twelve pack ago." I stood and helped her up out of her chair, and we stumbled to her door.

"Yeah, cake would be good. It wouldn't by chance be a sponge cake, would it?" I chuckled as I closed the door behind us. My plan was to eat cake, help Charlie to her bed, and then head home to my own. No doubt I would sleep like the dead.

CM Books, LLC

# Chapter Ten

## Moose

I walked up to the truck parked down the street from Kathryn's place. When I reached the opened window, Taylor stuck his head out.

"Brother, where is your bike?"

"Just so happens, our VP lives two blocks over. I parked at his house and walked here. See anything since you got here?" I asked.

Latch had called me right after I got back to my place and said an SUV drove by Kathryn's place twice but then never came around again. Latch figured the driver made him considering he was walking by the front of the place when whoever it was passed the first time.

He had parked around the corner where he could still see the place. But he'd gotten out to walk around the block to stretch his legs. He hadn't been worried Kathryn would spot him because even if she did, she wouldn't know who he was. So when he noticed the SUV that had come down the street, he acted like he was just out for a walk, and didn't look directly at the driver of the SUV. He watched it go by from the corner of his eyes and happened to recognize the driver. After seeing the SUV there, he also recalled that it had driven by the hospital last night, but he hadn't gotten a good look then or thought about the SUV until it made its round in front of Kathryn's place. My plan to force her dad's hand looked better by the minute.

"Convenient," Taylor said, his head turned up then down the street before coming back to me. "Latch filled me in when I got here. I was parked where he had his vehicle, but these yahoos were throwing a party, so I moved closer and blended in with all the cars parked here. They came back just a few minutes ago but only did one pass. No way they saw me sitting in the truck because a bunch of people was milling up and down the street going to the party. That might have been why they only went by once. You want me to stay here with you tonight?"

Taylor was going to make a great man to have at Haven after he was voted in, which would be soon. The only reason Wild Bill had held off was due to the shit with Stone. He wanted something good to celebrate the new beginning for Haven.

"Nah, no sense in both of us losing sleep," I said, and then another voice joined the mix.

"You could always try walking up to the door and ringing the bell. When she answers the door, kiss the hell out of her." I didn't even turn to look at Hawk while he spoke. Taylor chuckled and started his truck.

CM Books, LLC

"Going to go home since you don't need me. If you change your mind give me a call." Hawk and I stepped back from the truck and Taylor pulled out of the spot.

"Do you disagree with how I would handle her?" Hawk was a go after what you want type guy. The man held nothing back and never felt the need to apologize for anything he said or did.

"Yeah, one time while you are using that method, it is going to be with a chick who has the ability to bring Kaden Cross to his knees." Hawk burst out laughing, and I grinned. Damn, I couldn't wait for it to happen to him.

"It's not like I don't want a woman with a backbone, but I don't want a ball-buster either." He did a fake shiver that had me snorting just picturing the type woman it would take to bring my VP and friend down.

"Let's walk around the block, it's getting dark enough that if she's looking out her window, she won't be able to make me out." We walked down past her house.

"Moose, you know with them watching her that you are going to have to get her someplace safe until the Feds at least have what they need in their hands to take Kosnoff down. Until then, she is vulnerable. We know who is watching her for Kosnoff now, but what happens after we get rid of them?"

I knew Hawk was right. Hell, I had at first thought just to kidnap her and make her dad think Kosnoff had done it. Then I'd even wondered what she would do if I had picked her up and brought her to my house and chained her to my bed. That image made me smile. Katie would raise holy hell. Thoughts of all the things I wanted to do with her was not helping with coming up with a plan of action, and it definitely wasn't helping with the tightening of pants. Geez, thank God it was getting dark. All I would need is Hawk noticing. I'd never live that shit down.

An idea popped into my head no sooner than we turned the corner, giving us the view of her and the neighbor's yards.

"Holy shit, brother," Hawk whispered and slowed his steps. There on the neighbor's patio sat my girl, but she wasn't who Hawk was staring at. His focus was on the petite redhead Katie was sitting with.

"Keep walking before they look our way." We kept an even pace up that side of the block until they left our view. They would come back into view from between the houses when we turned the next corner. By the time we walked around the block and were on our way back to the street her house was on, I had a plan. One that would keep us from having to continue walking and chance the women spotting us.

When I mentioned it to Hawk, he agreed. So after we looked up and down the street and didn't see anyone, we cut into the yard and circled to the back from Kathryn's side because we knew we would be out of the women's sight. If we kept our voices low and with the two car garage as a divider, they wouldn't be able to hear us. The only way they would bust us was if they came around the back of the garage, but as loud as they were talking, we'd have plenty of time to move.

Hawk shook his head, and I smiled. There was no need for words. There would be two pissed off women if they knew we were listening to them talk. And unfiltered it would seem since they thought they were alone.

Should we have felt bad about eavesdropping on the women? Probably, but with all the things I heard, I couldn't bring myself to care. I thought it was going to be a rough road winning Kathryn back so hearing her talk to the woman she called Charlie about her and I growing up together I knew then if I played it right, she would be mine sooner than what I thought.

I didn't know how much time passed, but we thought we were busted for sure when Kathryn said she'd be right back that she was going home to get the cake. Hawk and I had moved so fast I was surprised they hadn't heard our footsteps because to me it sounded like horses stomping on the ground. We'd just made it around the corner of the house when I peeked around the outside wall and saw her step onto the patio that led to her back door.

She looked as beautiful now as she had the day of her graduation, and it sucked that she was close to me and I couldn't touch her. At least not yet. Soon though, because after seeing her again and being this close, it struck me what a fool had been to walk away.

"We will never live it down if we get picked up for being peeping Toms. You know that, don't you?" Hawk whispered, and I bit the inside of my cheek to keep from laughing out loud.

CM Books, LLC

"Ah, but they would love your pretty face in lockup." He punched me in the kidney, and I grabbed the corner of the wall to keep from falling out into the backyard and into full view.

The door opened and Kathryn walked out carrying the cake in one hand as she reached behind and pulled the door close.

"What the fuck, the woman doesn't lock her door?" I mumbled.

Hawk *shhhhst* me and only luck could be thanked for Kathryn not hearing us. When she was out of sight, we moved back to the patio and I tried the knob. Sure enough the door opened. I looked over at Hawk, and he shook his head.

I closed the door and left it unlocked. I would use her lack of safety and give Katie Stevens a little surprise.

Hawk stayed with me and we listened for a while longer. The longer we stood around, the louder the women got. I was just about to go over and tell Kathryn it was late and she needed to get her ass home when the woman Charlie started talking about the first time she'd ridden on the back of a motorcycle. Hawk inched around to the back of the garage so he could hear better, and so did I. If the brothers saw us there'd be no peace. They would never let us live this down. I was sure neither Hawk or I had acted like this even as teenage boys. Talk about stooping to a lower level.

"Girl, that ride is what turned me on to motorcycles. I'd gotten on behind Rocky, wrapped my arms around him, and when he revved that engine and the pipes rattled and the

CM Books, LLC

vibrations went through the bitch seat, my pussy tightened. I was instantly turned on. Hell, we rode around our town, and I found myself scooting back and forth on that seat searching for my release. I felt Rocky's stomach vibrate with laughter because he knew what I was doing. The jerk. We hit a stoplight, and he yelled at me over his shoulder to hold on and he would find a place to pull over, then he would help me get off. As we sat there waiting for the light to change, which by the way that had to be the longest freaking damn red light in history, another bike pulled up and Rocky must have known the man because he called him Chief Two Hairs.

"Anyway, he yells over the sound of both bikes and tells Rocky he needs to get his girl somewhere and take care of business because he'd been watching for the last little bit behind us and knew there had to be a snail trail on the seat. By the time we got to a spot off the beaten path, I should have finished my orgasm on the bike seat. Being bent over the handlebar is said to be sexy as hell, and it might be, but I'm sure the guy behind you needs to have a good-sized dick at least. The only thing I felt from Rocky was a little tickle that did nothing for me. He finished and when we got back on that bike, I closed my eyes and let that vibration take me to the best orgasm I've ever had. Snail trail hell, I left a stream on that seat. Damn, if I could find a guy with a dick that could please me like that, I don't think I'd ever stop riding him."

When Charlie finished, I could hear Kathryn laughing but that all stopped when Hawk lost his footing, smacked the garage wall, and the soft thud of his body along with my

113

"dumbass" as I reached out and grabbed his arm to keep him from falling was heard. Hell, if the women hadn't heard us, I was going to suggest hearing tests for both of them.

Everything went quiet, then we could hear whispers but couldn't make out what they were saying. Hawk looked at me and shook his head.

"Lockup here we come," he whispered, and I held my finger to my lips to quiet him. We heard shuffling and more low voices and then a door close. "They went in. We should probably get the hell out of here. I hope they didn't go in to get a gun," Hawk said.

"I'm staying, you go ahead and go home." Hawk's lips turned up on one side.

"Finally going to take my advice and kiss the hell out of her, aren't you?"

Damn, we had stepped back years in age. I glared at Hawk.

"Go home. No sense in both of going to jail if they call the cops. Besides, Katie left her door open, and I'm not going anywhere until I make sure she gets in okay."

"Okay, but your ass better not end up in jail. When you get ready to call it a night, your bike is in the garage at the house. You know where the key is." Hawk turned and walked away. He went out of sight around the corner, and I stepped into Kathryn's place. When she came home and found me there, going to lockup actually could be my reality.

# Chapter Eleven

## Katie

The light over the stove was on when I walked in the kitchen, and it kept me from tripping over the bar stools. I was glad I turned it on before I went back to Charlie's with the cake even if I didn't remember doing it. I sat the cake container down on the bar and looked around the room, nothing was out of place. Maybe I should have taken Charlie up on her offer to come to check my place out with me. But in her inebriated state, I wasn't sure she would be much help.

I turned back to the door and locked it, then went down the hall to double check the lock on the front door. As I passed the living room, I checked it too, everything looked fine. Geez, I felt jumpy, and I was sure it was because I wasn't as steady on my feet either from the beer Charlie and I drank

"Get a grip," I mumbled and started up the stairs after I kicked my shoes off. I picked them up to carry to my room. I found if I put away as I went, I didn't have to spend the majority of my time off cleaning. The nightlight at the end of the hall helped me to see the landing at the top of the stairs and the doorway to my room, which was good.

I pushed the door to my room the rest of the way open and walked straight to the nightstand. I felt around until I found the base of the lamp, then followed it to the switch and clicked it on. My shoes hit the floor, and the scream that escaped would probably have everyone in the neighborhood beating on my door or calling the police.

"Geez, Kathryn, I'd like to keep my hearing."

I closed my mouth and looked at the man sitting up in my bed as though he belonged there, which he didn't.

"Get the fuck out of my bed, Linc!"

"What? No hello first, sugar?"

The smile on his face was the same as the one I remembered, but his face was more chiseled now, fuller. His chest was bare except for the tat over his heart, the one he'd gotten when he turned eighteen: a heart with the ribbon going through it that held our initials. It was the only one he had then. Now, though, they ran down both arms. Arms that bulged with muscles and an eight-pack partially covered with my sheet. His hair was still brown with a hint of gold like it had been kissed by the sun. He was wearing it longer than he used to but his eyes, they were the same green that I had once loved to get lost in. They sparkled when he was happy or amused just as they did now as he looked me over.

"Hello? You want a hello? Okay. Hello, Linc. Now get the fuck out of my bed!"

CM Books, LLC

"You seem a little upset," he said as he continued to grin. I could never stay mad at him, and it seemed not to have changed. Maybe the mad was why I couldn't move on in the first place. I walked to the bedroom door and turned back toward him.

"You don't belong here, Linc. Get out of my bed and leave." Saying the words were nothing compared to the feelings coursing through my body. His silence made it twice as hard to stay firm.

"Come here, Katie." His voice lowered when he spoke, and the grin was gone from his face, replaced with regret reflecting back at me.

"Linc, it's late, and I've been drinking. Though I had a nice buzz going, you've taken that away. Even sober, I'm not sure I'm ready to do this right now."

I didn't move, and he didn't either. The man made me mad and want at the same time. I could hate him for that alone.

"Come. Here."

I stood my ground and didn't move. If I gave in, accepted him back in my life and he left me behind again... I wouldn't survive a second time.

"Out of the bed, Linc." I used the same low tone as he had before. He tilted his head and continued to stare at me. Minutes went by, and then in one fluid movement he was out of the bed and standing completely naked beside it. Where in hell were his clothes? I looked over to the chair in the corner, and there they were, along with his boots sitting on the floor beside it.

CM Books, LLC

"I'm out of bed. Now come here."

"Have you lost your mind?" It all had to be a dream. I would wake in the morning like every other time I had dreamt of him.

"No," was his only response.

"Just no? You break into my house. Strip and climb into my bed. And that is normal?" He took a step toward me and my breath hitched. God, he was a beautiful man.

"I didn't break into your house. You left the door unlocked. And you didn't even have a light on so you would be able to see when you walked in. No, you were just going to walk into a dark ass house that you had left unlocked for anyone degenerate to walk in. Be glad it was me."

"Well, that's debatable. Besides, this neighborhood is safe. I'm honestly surprised the cops haven't shown up since I screamed so loud."

"Me either," he said and took yet another step toward me.

"Stop!" I threw my arm out straight and held my hand's palm up in the stop sign.

"No."

Another step closer he moved.

"Would you stop saying no and put your clothes on?" I backed up until I touched the door.

"If looking at me like that, this is going to be fast, instead of me getting to take my sweet time with you. I've missed you, Katie." I refused to acknowledge the last, and it could've been because my eyes were mesmerized by his hand stroking up and down his erection.

118

"How the hell am I supposed to stop looking at you? That thing needs its own zip code." When I looked back up to his face, it had a smirk on it. Cocky bastard. I also noticed that he'd moved closer. He was almost in touching distance. And I wasn't going to kid myself that if he touched me, any resolve I held would vanish.

"Glad to know you still like it. Can't tell you how much I've missed you, Katie."

I opened my mouth to tell him that he couldn't have missed me too much or he would have come back to me, but I didn't get it out before he placed a hand on each cheek, tilted my face up, and set his mouth on mine. Even though I was five nine, he still had to bend his head down to reach me. His six foot five frame made me feel dainty. I wondered briefly what he would think of the changes in my body. It had changed from the body of a teenage girl and into a woman's with curves and dips. He deepened the kiss; it went from soft to demanding as he pushed his tongue in and tasted every crevice of my mouth. I didn't want to participate in the kiss, but as he took what he wanted, I realized I wanted it, too.

I melted into him. My body pressed flush against his. I felt his cock twitch between us as its hardness pressed against my stomach. The door shut as he pushed me back against it.

When Linc broke the kiss, I was left breathless as he worked his way down my neck, kissing, nipping the skin as he found the tender spot between my neck and shoulder. His hands dropped from my cheeks to my shoulders and made

119

their journey down my arms taking the straps of my tank with them. The top moved down, and my breasts were freed, leaving nothing in his way as he moved down until his mouth reached a nipple. His tongue circled and then sucked the now peaked nipple into his mouth and bit gently, causing a shiver to work its way through my body. The pop was heard as he released it and moved to the other one, giving it ample attention.

His hands reached mine, and he grabbed them pushing my arms up and over my head. He released the breast he had been worshipping and stepped back, leaving me to feel the loss of his heat.

Linc pulled my shirt up until it was over my head and my arms, then he tossed it on the floor. My jeans were undone and off along with my panties, and I was left standing against the door naked before him. His eyes were roaming my body.

"Damn, you are beautiful." When his eyes met mine, my vision was blurred by tears that had filled my eyes. Not sure if I was upset because he still knew how to control my body or the fact I had felt so much since he left me.

The tears escaped and began to run down my cheeks. Linc bent and lifted me into his arms and carried me to the bed and laid me down. I watched him as he walked to the chair and when he returned, he set the condoms he had retrieved from his jeans on the nightstand and then joined me on the bed.

"I'll stop if that is what you really want. My intentions were good, Katie, now and when I left you. But I hurt you and I don't want to do it again." He held his body over mine, rested on his elbows and used the thumbs on his hands to wipe the tears from my cheeks.

As I looked into his green eyes, I saw the truth of his words. He left the final decision up to me. Could I let everything go? Wasn't it time? And God, I wanted him.

At my nod, he bent his head until our mouths met. The kiss brief as he again made his way down my body, stopping only at my breasts to give each a kiss before he continued to work his way down my body. When he hit my belly button, his tongue circled and dipped in, then he licked and kissed his way from one hipbone to the other.

I'd never felt so worshiped in my life, not even when he and I had sex before. But we'd been young. Inexperienced. What a difference it made from being horny teens to adults who knew the benefit of exploring and using it as Linc was doing.

My body burned from the inside. I felt each pulse as my heart picked up speed. The goosebumps that were left behind as he moved lower.

My hands that laid on the bed, grasped the sheets as his mouth worked its way between my legs. The first swipe of his tongue through my folds had my back arching off the bed.

Linc lifted my legs over his shoulders, giving himself more room. His tongue pierced through, and I was caught off guard by how fast the orgasm hit. My body shook while he continued his assault on me. No sooner as I began to settle, he sucked my clit and bit gently, rocking my system

121

until another orgasm consumed me. My fingers dug into the sheets as I tried to hold on while he continued to work me.

When my body settled once again, he raised his head, removed my legs from his shoulders, and laid them gently on the bed, leaving me spread wide as he worked his way back up my body.

I finally released the sheets to run my hands through his hair, damp from his efforts, then moved them down his arms, his back, anywhere I could reach. His skin was soft, but the muscles underneath that bulged and strained against it were hard. He hadn't been filled out when we'd laid in his bed while our parents were out for the night. But he had been an attentive young lover, though. On the one hand, I wanted to push him away, hurt him how he'd hurt me. Instead, I pulled him so close that I felt as though I was a part of him.

Finding him in my bed had not only brought the painful memories of him leaving, but they had also brought the memories of every day he and I had spent together before he left. I realized the past needed to be just that, the past. I wanted to reach for my future. Linc had been and always would be a part of me. I wasn't sure I wanted to let him go.

The crinkle of paper brought me back just as he pulled away to roll the condom on. Once he on, he placed his hands on each side of me and leaned down to kiss my lips. When he raised back up, he looked down at me and with one of his hands, touched my cheeks.

"I don't ever want to make you cry again, Katie."

"I'm not sure they were sad tears, Linc. Maybe more like I can't believe you are really here tears." For the first time since finding him in my bed, I smiled at him.

"I can't wait any longer to be inside you," he said and waited for me to give him permission. His erection resting against my entrance. Him giving me a choice meant more to me at that moment than anything else.

"Then don't wait. I've waited a long time for you to come back to me." The words had barely left my mouth when I felt him break through. He rolled his hips and thrust, settling deeper inside me. Then he'd pull back out and begin again.

"You're so goddamn tight. When I fill you, I'm not going to last very long."

While he labored to work himself into me, I explored his body with my hands until he shifted enough to run a hand between us. He spread his hand over my mound and pressed the thumb against my clit. He moved it back and forth until I arched my back, then raised my hips to meet his. The move gave him what he needed and pushed into the hilt with just that one more movement of his hips.

Linc stilled to give me enough time to adjust to his size. The time needed so I could relax around him.

"I gotta move, babe." Linc pulled back, then slammed in. Each time pausing, each time filling me until I felt the small bite of pain. The pace he had set was torture. I grabbed his ass to hold him in place. When that didn't work, I clawed his back each time he filled me.

"Please, Linc. I need more," I wasn't ashamed to beg. I needed the friction for the orgasm that was eluding me.

"Hang on. The tightness and warmth of your pussy are already working on me." He gritted his teeth and thrust back in.

"I need it harder. Damn it, Linc, fuck me!"

He pushed his body up and held his weight on one arm while his other moved down until he gripped my thigh. He lifted it up and placed it bent at his hip and started to move—each thrust harder than the one before.

"Put your hands on the headboard, I don't want you to hit your head." Before I could reply, Linc began a pace that had the bed moving with his motion. When he slammed into me, the headboard banged the wall. If I had to have the wall repaired who cared because as our hips met, his pelvic bone rubbed my clit, and then on the next pass he rolled his hips and I saw stars behind my eyes.

The combined feelings racked my body until I slung my head back, arched my back, and screamed his name as I climaxed.

As I came down from my bliss, I couldn't believe the man hadn't gone over the edge with me, and I opened my eyes and looked at him. His focus was where we were joined, and he watched himself exit and enter me.

Linc's eyes lifted to mine, and he spoke through gritted teeth, "Fuck me, I can't get enough."

"I am fucking you, or you are fucking me," I said as my breath came out labored.

CM Books, LLC

"Funny," he said, and before I knew it, he pulled out, flipped me to my stomach, and entered me from behind. The new angle had his sack hitting my clit each time he bottomed out. I was going to be sore the next day, but no way would I regret it.

The pounding he was giving me lasted long enough for me to feel the tingling of yet another orgasm building. It would be a miracle if I survived another one. None of this could be real. I expected to wake and find I'd only dreamt about him. Again.

Linc squeezed my hips, made a final thrust, then draping his body over mine and went we over the edge together.

"Damn, I thought for a minute we were going to break the fucking bed," Linc said as he fell to the side bringing me with him.

I made an unladylike snort while I worked to even out my breath. Linc did the same. Both of us quiet as we laid there connected.

When his cock twitched and began to harden once more, I tried to shift away. "Oh, hell no. Get that thing out. Geez."

I felt his body vibrate behind me, then the loss of him as he slipped out and rose off the bed.

"Be back, need to get rid of the condom."

I turned the light out, then closed my eyes and started to dose until a warm cloth was placed between my legs. Linc cleaned me up, put the washcloth in the bathroom, and slid into the bed. He pulled me close and wrapped me in his arms.

"We need to talk, Linc," I said with a sleep filled voice.

"I know. Tomorrow, babe. Let's not ruin what we shared." I felt him kiss the top of my head.

"Missed you, Linc."

"I missed you, too, babe. And not sure if I actually knew how much until now."

It was quiet, and sleep started to pull me under when I heard Linc whisper.

"I may never deserve you, Katie. But I'll never let you go again."

# Chapter Twelve

## Moose

The first thing I sensed before I even opened my eyes was that I was alone in the bed. I stretched my arm out to feel the sheets where Katie laid last night, and they were cold. As I rolled on my back, the smell of coffee and bacon enveloped me. At least I knew where she was.

I got up and went to the bathroom, and when I walked out, she was there, standing with a cup in her hand. Her hair was rumpled, and she had thrown on shorts and a t-shirt. The smile she wore lit up her face, and as I looked at her, I understood for the first time what the phrase '*the look of a well-loved woman*' meant.

"Please tell me that is for me," I said and leaned on the doorframe leading out of the bathroom.

"Yes, I also have bacon, toast, and eggs ready, too. Interested?" I pushed off the frame and walked to her.

"Yeah, in a lot of things." I removed the cup from her hand and set it on the dresser, then wrapped my arms around her and pulled her into me. I leaned down and took her mouth. She tasted like coffee mixed with mint. I could have moaned.

I kissed her until I felt her go soft in my arms and when I broke the kiss, my erection pressed into her stomach. I wanted nothing more than to haul her back to bed and spend the day inside her, but after last night and then the two other times I'd woken; it wouldn't have surprised me if she'd been unable to walk.

Releasing her, I stepped back, grabbed the cup of coffee and swallowed a huge gulp, enjoying the jolt of that first taste.

"Good grief, Linc, can you put that thing away."

I glanced down at my dick that pointed straight at her. "He wanted to say hello this morning, but you'd already gotten out of bed."

"After last night and early this morning, I'm surprised he can still respond."

"Don't have any issues in that department, sweetheart. Just ignore him." I lifted the cup to my lips to take a drink as Katie stepped closer.

When she wrapped her hand around my dick, I swallowed the liquid in my mouth, then groaned.

"Shit, babe, unless you want me to throw you on that bed and sink balls deep into you again, you might want to let him go."

Katie dropped to her knees and her tongue came out and circled the head. Christ, she gave no warning, and I had just enough time to set the cup down before I spilled the

CM Books, LLC

steaming coffee on us both. I leaned my ass against the dresser because I needed the support.

Katie ran her tongue along the underside from base to tip, then circled the head. A drop of pre-cum began to roll down the side, and her tongue came out and scooped it up like it was ice cream about to drip on the side of a cone.

With one hand as close wrapped around my dick, she took her other hand and began to play with my balls. Her mouth opened wide, and she took me in.

My hands went to her hair, and with a hand on each side of her head, I took over and held her still while I stood so I could thrust my hips. I fucked her mouth and knew she was as turned on as I was when she moaned. The vibrations went all the way down into my balls.

"You enjoying my dick?" I took the next moan as yes. The hand she still had on my balls began to roll them around, and when her finger touched, then stroke the underside, my knees almost buckled.

I couldn't take my eyes off where I tunneled in and out of her mouth. When the tingle started, I knew I was close.

"I don't want to come in your mouth, babe. So pull that shirt you're wearing off, I want to shoot on those beautiful breasts." She hummed and that was all it took. "Fuck, now!" I let go of her head and pulled out of her mouth.

Katie yanked her shirt up and over her head. The sight of her peaked nipples told me she'd been really into me fucking her mouth. With my hand, I only had to stroke my cock twice before cum sprayed all over her breasts. I watched a shiver go through her, and she tightened her thighs. She was primed. I pumped until every drop was wrung out of my dick. It might make me an asshole, but I liked her wearing my mark. I reached down and helped her up, her breasts glistening.

Once I walked her back to the edge of the bed, I pushed her down and back until she laid on the bed with her legs dangling over the edge. I knelt and grabbed the waist of her cotton shorts and ripped them down her legs, and damn if my baby hadn't gone commando. I placed her legs over my shoulders and my mouth on her center. When I saw her watching me, I pulled away.

"Open for me, babe." She moved her legs on my shoulders like she was trying to give me more room. "No, babe. Reach between your legs and hold those pretty lips open for me. Offer yourself to me. I see your juices waiting for me to lap them up."

She paused at first as if she wasn't going to do it.

"You don't want to feel my tongue run through your lips, or me sucking your clit?" I lifted a brow.

Her hands came down and she used her fingers to spread herself wide. I would have chuckled at the speed if the smell of her arousal wasn't filling my head.

I leaned in and licked her from back to front and then did it again. I fucked her with my tongue. Her knees were beginning to press into my ears, and her hips thrust up and rolled as she tried to chase my tongue to get it where she needed.

CM Books, LLC

After one more swipe, I moved my focus to her clit. My tongue circled it, and I knew that was going to send her over the edge when her hips pushed back, needing just a little more. My dick was hard as steel again from her moaning and thrashing on the bed. I moved my hand to her mound and used the thumb to rub circles and keep the pressure on her clit. When her head bowed back, I knew she was ready. I stood, lined myself at her entrance, and slammed into the hilt.

Katie was beautiful to watch as her body convulsed and shook, her back arched, her head thrown back as her orgasm rolled through. When her body settled down, I pulled out, picked her up, and carried her to the bathroom to get cleaned up.

"Breakfast is gonna be cold," she said and rested her head on my chest.

"That's what microwaves are for, sweetheart," I said and kick the door closed behind us.

We'd showered, dressed, ate the breakfast she'd fixed earlier, and were now sitting side by side on the couch in her living room. It seemed the time to talk was upon us.

"It's tomorrow, Linc," Katie said as she fidgeted in her seat with her hands resting in her lap.

"I know. What do you want to hear first?" I asked, and she shifted on the couch to face me.

"Why you left me? Why didn't you come back for me? Then why all of a sudden, I became important enough for you to break into my house? You can start with any of those." I watched her big brown eyes fill with tears, and my chest squeezed. When we got through this, I never wanted to see her cry again. I couldn't take Katie upset.

I took a deep breath and began, "I was eighteen, getting ready to turn nineteen and had no idea what I wanted, except you. It scared the hell out of me. I didn't want to go to college and work at our dads' firm. And before you say that I'm smart, let me finish. I know my IQ is off the charts and I could have been anything I wanted if I'd gone to college. Yeah, I could have had a job making tons of money, stayed right here, waited until you were of age and married you, had a few kids, but I would have never felt complete."

Her tears started to run down her face, and I realized she thought I didn't want to do all that with her.

Shit.

"Stop. You would have been the only good part of that scenario." I reached over with both hands and used my thumbs to wipe the tears from her cheeks before I continued. "Let me start at the very beginning. I left you so you could grow up and fulfill the dreams you had. Katie, you'd always wanted to be a doctor, and you wouldn't have been if I had stayed."

"You don't know that! You didn't give us a try, you just bailed!" I smiled, that yelling and standing up to me was part of the girl I left behind—the one who knew what she wanted and reached out and took it.

"Yeah, I do. Oh, you would have said you were going to go, then a kid would have come along and you would have kept postponing going to college. After that, it would have

CM Books, LLC

been too late, and resentment would have come between us. Yours, because you didn't reach your dream, and mine, because I would have been working a job I hated just to have you."

Couldn't she see I did it all to save us?

"I got over the part where you left, Linc. It took a while, but I threw myself into my schoolwork to keep you out of my head. It became easier because I focused on the one part of your goodbye. You said you would come back for me. That's what got me through college and med school. Instead, you stayed away. Then when you did come back, we avoided each other like the plague."

I rubbed a hand over the back of my neck. "I planned to keep that promise. I did actually, but when I showed up, you looked so happy and then when you hugged the guy that was there at the end of graduation. Well, I didn't want to take that away from you." I shrugged and shook my head. That day I had left, went back to the home I had built just for her, and drank to forget.

"You left because I looked happy? What fucking guy?" Katie stood from the couch and moved to stand in front of me. "What man?!" she yelled.

"Alexi Viktor Kosnoff. You would know him as Charles Alexander. It's the name he uses when he's in public."

"My dad's client? The one doing all the illegal shit?"

"Yes. His business associates call him Kosnoff, but his full name is Alexi Viktor Kosnoff. Katie, he's wanted for a lot of things. Ugly things. More than what he had Paul doing for him."

"Did you know all this the day of my graduation? I don't understand, Linc. My father invited him; he even came to the party my parents threw afterward."

"No! Do you think I would have left you if I had known?"

"No. But are you here now because you do?"

I wanted to grab her and turn her over my knee for even thinking for a moment that I left her in the hands of a human trafficker. But I couldn't, she had the right to think the worst. I had handled everything wrong with her from the beginning. That stopped now.

"Listen to me. I fucked up that day. I should have stayed. I should have taken what was mine, but I didn't. Now, I've been handed the opportunity again with all this mess, but I would have come for you eventually, Katie. Everything I have done my whole life has been so I could have you in the end. I just took the long way around to get to this moment."

"Linc Harris, I want to smack the crap out of you and kiss you at the same time." Between the words that came out her mouth and the look on her face, a chuckled escaped before I could hold it back.

I smirked and asked, "Which one is winning?" Because I never knew when to shut up.

"Right now, smacking the crap out of you. I can't believe you have the nerve to laugh."

"How about you go with the second one? Be the bigger person between the two of us." The grin I wore was wiped off my face when she lunged at me, knocking my breath out as she landed. Katie positioned herself on my lap and then grabbed my face in her hands and bent until her forehead touched mine.

"At graduation, I was happy. But it wasn't because of Charles being there. I was happy because all my dreams were coming true that day. I was going to be a doctor, which was one. But the other, it was because I expected you to come and claim me as yours. You, Linc, were the main reason I was happy that day."

When she finished talking, she kissed me. It didn't take long until we were both breathless. She broke the kiss, moved her hands from my face to my chest, and through my shirt she grabbed both nipples and twisted.

"Owww. What the fuck was that for?" I moved my hands from her waist to rub out the pain.

"Don't you ever make a decision for me again? We make them together. We'll never know how things might have worked out if you had stayed instead of leaving. But that is our past, and we'll have to live with it. Right now is where we need to focus." She kissed my lips and slid off my lap and sat beside me.

"Hey, come back here." I reached for her, and she scooted away.

"Uh no, because while I was talking I noticed something and he is not coming out to play for a while, I'm sore." When Katie said that, she looked at my crotch and the

135

bastard twitched and made my pants move slightly. I smirked at the look on her face.

"I can control him. But don't blame him for getting hard since your ass was wiggling around on him. And you're going to have to get used to it because when you're around, he'll more than likely stay that way. We can hold off so you can heal."

She scooted beside me and leaned her head against my arm. I shifted until my arm was around her and she was tucked against me. We sat quietly for a while and I hated to break the peace, but there was something we needed to discuss.

"Katie, about condoms?"

She sighed and turned her face up toward me. "I know we had unprotected sex a couple of times. I'm on the pill, however, I know I've not been the only woman you have been with. Are you clean, Linc?"

For a doctor, she almost looked a little embarrassed to ask. "I'm clean. And don't be embarrassed for asking. I get tested every six months even though I've never skipped wearing a condom before. Though I'll admit I've not been a saint, I'm not going to talk about other women either. You are the only woman that has ever mattered to me." I reached for my wallet, and once I had it in my hands, I opened it and pulled out a folded piece of paper and handed it to her. She took it and opened it.

"This is recent?"

"Like I said, twice a year. The General requires it because we go out of the country once in a while. But we

136

would do it anyway with the club." Her brows furrowed and it hit me she would know nothing about either of those. "What do you want to know, sweetheart? I can almost hear the wheels turning in your head. And keep in mind I can't tell you everything because some things are confidential and the other deals with club business."

She rolled her eyes. "Why don't you just tell me what you can? It would probably be easier. Start at where you went when you left, up to now with Haven. I know you've probably been a lot of places and seen a lot of things. I've been nowhere other than school. I'd like to experience what you did—through your eyes."

"Okay, but trust me, not everything or place would be something you would want to see or an area to vacation." I talked and told her about my time in the military, then how after I came back, I rode around looking for a place to call home. She listened without interruption as I caught her up on everything with me from the day I left to up until now.

"You found a home with Haven?" she asked.

"Yes, they're my brothers. I would die for them just as I would for you or my parents."

"And signing up as an anti-terrorist agent? How does that work?"

"Wild Bill and a few of the others had started it with General Patel. Patel had been a lieutenant in Wild Bill's unit. The General was approached about a new program the government wanted to start where ex-military with specialties are hired and paid per the job they do. Our job is to go into the city, or even country, where they have picked up activity

CM Books, LLC

on terrorist cells, drug trafficking, and any other criminal activity they need handled with the least amount of flash. Things they'd like to keep low profile and out of the news. It is like the app everyone is playing where they hunt Pokémon and then capture them. We're the human version. We actually leave for a job in a couple of weeks. I can't tell you where, though."

"If this works out—"

I cut her off. "There is no working it out, Katie. As far as I'm concerned, that is what we just did here. You are mine. You're my ol' lady."

"Your, what did you call it?"

"My ol' lady? Yeah, that is what you are."

"I told you not to make decisions for me again."

"I didn't. You made that decision." It was as if I could see the wheels turning in her head.

"I did no such thing!" Yeah, my woman was gearing up for a fight that she wouldn't win.

"Last night when you let me in your bed, and I took your body. Your future was sealed."

"I didn't let you in my bed. If you recall, you were already there." My lips twitched when she crossed her arms over her chest.

"You didn't kick me out either."

"I did; you just wouldn't leave!"

"Don't blame it on a technicality."

"You're a cocky bastard, Linc Harris."

"You know what?" I asked, and she glared at me.

"What?" Katie sighed, and I grinned.

"I'm your cock-y bastard." I chuckled as she bowed her head.

"So it would seem," she mumbled, and I flat out laughed, then pulled her into my arms.

CM Books, LLC

CM Books, LLC

# Chapter Thirteen

## Katie

Linc and I stayed behind the locked doors of my place for two days without the outside world interfering. The only visitor had been one of Linc's brothers he called Hawk. I didn't get to meet him. I just knew that the doorbell rang and Linc answered, only to grab the bag of clothes and essentials he had his friend bring by for him. Heck, I hadn't even known he'd called the man.

We hadn't had sex since that first night and morning because I'd been too sore. Instead, we just slept curled up in each other arms, relearning about each other all over again.

The peace and quiet ended the third morning when Linc's phone rang on the nightstand. I laid across his chest and listened as he talked with his prez on the cell in his one hand while the other rubbed up and down on my back.

"Well, we knew they were going to move on that pretty quick. No shit? Any idea where they went? Yeah, I'd put money on that, too. Uh huh, I'll be there. I'm going to bring Katie with me. She will. Not sure, but there's nothing I can do about that. Yeah, I'll check with him and see if they found what we needed to know and fill you in after we get there. Oh yeah, left that at Hawk's. Can you have Taylor and Sparks drive over, then one can ride it here? Great. See you in a bit." Linc hung up and set his phone back on the nightstand.

"You have to go to the clubhouse?" I asked.

"We need to have Church. You're going to go with me, though."

I raised up so I could see his eyes. "I don't need to go, Linc. You have business to talk about. I'll stay here, and you can come back when you're done."

Even dealing with people every day in my job, I was nervous about meeting Linc's brothers and the other ol' ladies of Haven. Not to mention the hang-arounds, as they called the women who dropped by for parties or slept with one or more of the members. Most only did it because they loved bad boys and bikers fit that build.

"You're going. The guys want to meet you, and besides, there's a party tonight so you will get to meet some of the ol' ladies and a lot of the other members. Plus, I don't want to leave you here alone. The phone call wasn't just about club business.

"The Feds moved on Kosnoff's Seattle office and the one in Canada combined with Canada's forces. He wasn't at either place, so they looked into if he had flown home to Russia. No record of him taking a plane, boat, or renting a jet. Nothing. So you go with me."

"I need to call my dad and see if he and Mom are doing okay and if he is cooperating with the Feds. Linc, he did some really bad things, but he did a lot of them out of fear of Kosnoff. Will they take that into consideration when deciding his fate?"

"I'm not sure. Dad said the last time I talked to him that they were meeting with an attorney who handles stuff like this. I guess it would depend on how much information your dad can supply and how cooperative he is with them."

"I still can't believe Kosnoff threatened my dad by holding my mom and me over his head."

"I told you, your mom was just that—a threat. You, on the other hand, were to be his next conquest, either his or he planned to put into the human trafficking ring."

A shiver ran through my body when I thought of that. "Have they located any information on the ring?"

"No, nothing yet. I gotta make a call and check on it. But we need to get up and get ready. A couple of the Prospects are going to pick my bike up at Hawk's and drop it off here. We'll ride it to the club. They'll grab an extra helmet from Hawk's for you to use."

"We could take my car. I haven't been the back of a bike since you bought your very first one." The look he gave me was strange, and the smirk that followed when I look at him didn't help. "What?"

"You sure it's not because you think you might leave a… snail trail on my seat?"

"Really, I can control myself. I can't even believe you would bring that…" My eyes went wide, and I paused. "Oh

143

my God, you were outside the other night listening to Charlie and I talk, weren't you?" His green eyes took on a sparkle, and his lips twitched. He so had been there.

"If I say no, will you believe it?"

I could only stare as Linc fought not to laugh. Jerk. "No!"

"Fine, we were but not the entire time."

"How long, Linc?"

"A couple of hours."

I threw my shirt at him. "There was more than just you? Seriously?" No way was I mentioning this to Charlie.

"Only Hawk. Quit worrying, no one is going to say anything. Now get moving. Prez doesn't like it when we're late, and we only have three hours before Church." He walked toward the bathroom, and I stared at his firm ass.

"Wait, three hours is plenty of time. Where is the clubhouse?" I asked, and he stopped in the doorway and turned to face me. When I looked down, his cock stood hard and was straining to the point the veins were pronounced.

"Clubhouse is ten minutes away, tops. But I'm going to need a good hour and a half for the things I'm going to do to you in the shower. Hope your hot water heater is a good one."

My lower region spasmed and I put my thighs together to try to ease the feeling. I watched him turn toward the shower and then reach in and turn on the water.

I pulled the shirt over and off and wiggled the shorts I'd worn to bed down my leg as I walked, leaving them where I stepped out of them.

CM Books, LLC

"I like water games," I said, kicking the door closed as he laughed.

# Moose

We heard the rumble of bikes as they pulled into the driveway. When Katie and I opened the door and walked out, Taylor had already parked my bike and was at the curb getting into the truck's passenger seat that Sparks was driving. I lifted my chin to them and they drove away. Hawk remained on his bike, and after I locked the front door, I put my hand in the small of Katie's back and led her to the driveway.

"Thought I'd follow the brothers over and check on you, Moose. Make sure you weren't buried in the backyard." I shook Hawk's hand and then turned to Katie.

"Your club name is Moose? I didn't even think to ask you what your road name is." She looked at me and then at Hawk, and when the pink tint rose on her face, I knew where her mind went.

"*That's* not why they call me Moose." I chuckled, and Hawk grinned at her.

"He picked that name up because he doesn't back down, he just charges forward. Like a Moose," Hawk explained to her.

"Oh," she said sheepishly, and I grinned.

"So… what did you think it was for?" Hawk asked her, and I saw his lips twitch.

CM Books, LLC

Hawk and the others were in for a surprise when she relaxed around them because she wouldn't cut them any slack and allow them to get away with shit.

To save Katie, I didn't give her a chance to reply to Hawk. "This derelict is Haven's VP, Hawk. Hawk, this is my ol' lady, Kathryn." Katie's head whipped in my direction, and I winked. "Might as well get used to it, babe." She shook her head and turned back to Hawk.

"Nice to meet you, Hawk. Are you as bullheaded as his ass?" Katie stuck her hand out, and Hawk shook it.

"Darlin', I'm worse."

Katie laughed. "Well, thanks for the warning."

"Ready? Wild Bill wants to get Church over with before the place fills up and the noise level rises."

"Yeah, I'm ready." I looked down at Katie. "You ready, sweetheart." She glanced at the bike, then back to me.

"Ready as I'm ever going to be."

I reached over and grabbed the helmet Taylor had strapped on and turned and handed it to her.

"Let me help you put it on." Just as I was about to place the helmet on her head, another bike rumble was heard, and then the bike in question turned the corner. The three of us watch as it moved down the street, then slowed and turned into the driveway next to Katie's and stopped.

The garage door started to rise, and by the time it was completely open, the woman was off her bike and shaking out her red hair as she placed her helmet on the seat.

"Sonofabitch," Hawk whispered and kept his eyes on the woman. I wanted to laugh because Hawk loved women,

CM Books, LLC

but as I watched this one glance in our direction, then start toward us—I didn't think she looked the type to go along with Hawk's way of going straight forward at what he wanted.

"Well damn, girl. Your ass has been holding out on me." The woman walked up to Katie, but her eyes roamed over Hawk and then me before she faced Katie.

"Hey, Charlie. This is Linc and..." I grinned at Katie because she didn't know if she should introduce Hawk as Hawk, but she didn't know his given name either.

"Kaden, babe. Hawk's name is Kaden." I looked at Hawk because he wasn't talking and that was unusual for him. Especially when it came to women.

"This is Linc and Kaden, Charlie, they are with Haven MC."

"Nice to meet you. I'm Charlie Rhoades." She stuck her hand out, and Hawk dismounted his bike and walked around it. He took her hand and shook it while he stared down at her.

"Good to meet you, too. What's is Charlie short for?" he asked her.

I watched the exchange and saw the interest in Hawk's eyes as he continued to look at only her.

"Nothing, just Charlie. My dad wanted a boy, so my mom compromised when I was born." Charlie shrugged, then frowned down to where Hawk still held her hand. She pulled her hand back, then shoved in her back pocket.

Sometimes the ability to read people came in handy, other times it was a burden. But as I watched Hawk slowly

147

drop his own hand and take a step back, I knew both were interested. However, I wondered how long it would take for one or the other to make a move.

When no one said anything else, I glanced at Katie who wore a small smile. Evidently, I wasn't the only one to pick up on the attraction. Deciding to cut us all a break, I cleared my throat, drawing Hawk's and Charlie's eyes toward me.

"It was nice to meet you, Charlie. You're going to have to come to the club with Katie sometime."

Charlie glanced at Hawk, then back to me. "You bet, if the others look like you two, I will definitely be there." Hawk smiled, and I chuckled. "I'll let you get going. I'm meeting my bosses to go over some things before I start work. Have a good time, hon. And a nice ride," Charlie said to Katie and turned toward her place without another word.

"Okay, let's get going before Prez starts blowing up our phones," I said and turned to put the helmet on Katie's head. Hawk mounted his bike and grabbed his own helmet to put on.

"I'll get on first, and then you get on behind me. You'll be fine, sweetheart. All you got to do is hold on to me." I grabbed my helmet Taylor had left hanging on one of the handlebars. As I stepped up to my bike, the sound of a vehicle approaching had me glancing over my shoulder to see a black SUV with tinted windows driving toward us. I shouted, "Incoming," and hoped it was loud enough for Hawk and Charlie to hear as the side window began to roll down.

"What the hell, Linc!" Katie yelled when I took us both to the ground.

"Keep your head down," I said and pushed on the back of the helmet she still wore. Hawk had heard me and jumped off his bike and did the same.

When I glanced in Charlie's direction, she too was on the ground. I looked back toward the SUV and watched as a bottle was hurled through the open window. The next heard was the sound of glass breaking as it hit its mark. I didn't have to look to know it was Katie's place that had taken the hit.

The gunfire I expected to hear next never came as the rumble of pipes growing louder had the SUV gunning away as fast as it had shown up. I angled my head to get a better look at who was riding on the bikes that probably saved lives. I could only make out four riders.

"Nice friends you have!!" Charlie yelled as she rose from the ground.

"Hey, they could have been yours?" Hawk yelled back as he pushed himself up off the ground.

"Sugar, I've not been here long enough to piss anyone off," Charlie said and began to dust off.

I stood and helped Katie up as the bikes stopped and four big men got off.

"Fuck, this isn't how you welcome people to this state," Charlie said as she met the men halfway.

I looked over at Hawk as Charlie spoke to the men and he shrugged. Both of us wondering how she knew the men.

"We were thinking you must be having a helluva party. At least it was until we this two guys." Mitchell, the one who answered Charlie, pointed his thumb in mine and Hawk's direction.

"Us? Trouble follows you everywhere, Mitchell," I said and stepped up and shook his hand. "Shit, man. I don't know what you four are doing here, but thanks."

The Matherson brothers owned and operated a bounty hunting company in the area. We'd met them when we started to clean up Haven and were checking every member out to see if they had any ties to Stone. There had been three we'd turned over to the bounties for skipping out on bail. They'd joined Haven only use the club to hide out.

"Think we can chit-chat after we move these bikes and get out of the way for the fire trucks?" Travis said, and the other men just shook their heads.

I heard the sirens, and they were close, probably called by one of Katie's neighbors. I looked at her place and the fire burning through her living room windows confirmed the direct hit and that whatever was in the Molotov cocktail thrown was highly flammable—likely gasoline or alcohol.

Katie put her arm around my waist and leaned against me. "I guess I'm going to need to move." I looked down at her as she'd pulled the helmet off, and some of her hair was sticking out from her ponytail. "Do you think we should move my car out of the garage?"

She was awfully calm, considering her home was in flames. I placed my arm around her and squeezed. "Got the keys on you, sweetheart?"

"No."

"Then we can only hope they get the fire out and it doesn't spread to the garage and damage your car. But, Katie, everything can be replaced."

"I know. Get your bike moved, Linc. I'll be alright."

I leaned over and kissed the top of her head and got on and started my bike. I moved it down the street where the others were parking theirs.

We started back toward Katie's house as the fire trucks pulled up. By the time I got to where Katie was standing, a few places down from hers, the firemen had their gear on, the truck hooked up to the fire hydrant at the corner and were already working on the fire.

"Katie needs to be somewhere safe because this was a desperate move," Hawk said as he walked up with the others. Beside me, Katie talked with Charlie and neither of them was paying attention to our conversation.

"Yeah, I could take her to my house, which I'd planned to do tonight, but until we catch the two in that SUV, I don't think she will be safe. This wasn't Kosnoff. He would have been a fuck of a lot more organized. He sure wouldn't have hit in broad daylight."

"Does your girl got trouble looking for her, Moose?" Travis said as he and his brothers joined us.

"Yeah, a little or a lot, depending on how you look at it. What the hell were you guys doing on this part of town?"

Travis threw his thumb in Charlie's direction. "Came to go over a few things with our new employee."

"No shit, did you guys finally hire a secretary at your place?" Hawk asked, and the men laughed.

"Nah, man, she's our new bounty hunter."

I should have had my phone ready to take a pic of Hawk's face. Even with everything going on around us, I missed getting Haven's VP caught off guard. With Hawk, it didn't often happen if ever, that he was shocked.

"Are you fucking kidding me? I haven't heard any news about there being a rash of kids who need to be pick up for breaking bail?" Hawk said as he looked over at Charlie.

"Man, don't let her hear you say that. We ran into her on a job in Philly and watched her take the knees out on this big motherfucker," Josh said as he glanced in Charlie's direction and then back at us.

Mine and Hawk's phones started to buzz before we could reply to Josh. I slid  mine out of my pocket and looked down at the screen to see Prez's text.

I hit the Prez's number in my contacts and waited for him to pick up. When he did, I filled him in on everything that had happened and told him as soon as we could, we would be at the clubhouse. The others were there, so he said once Hawk and I made there, then Church would be held. I hung up and walked back to where everyone stood, having moved away to talk to my prez.

"Are you in trouble for missing Church?" Katie said as she moved beside me and laid her head on my arm, still watching the firemen.

"No, babe. We'll have our meeting when Hawk and I get there."

"Okay."

"You going to be okay, sweetheart?"

"Yeah, just not looking forward to looking for a new place to live. I like this place."

I pulled her around until she faced me. This was as good as time as any. "You're moving in with me. And don't say it's too soon. We've waited long enough to be together. I want to wake in the morning with you beside me and fall asleep with you each night."

Her eyes filled with tears as she looked up at me. "I love you, Linc. I always have, but I'm not sure moving this fast is the answer. What if we were never supposed to end up together? What if the only reason we've reconnect is because of what my father has done?"

"Enough, Katie. I'm not going to second guess the reason. I would have made my way back to you. I've loved you since I was eight years old, dammit. I was stupid to walk away and will regret for the rest of my life." I leaned down and took her mouth and kissed her as whistles and catcalls were yelled in the background.

I might have been a fool before, but I was smarter now, and the life I wanted with her was just around the corner. And I would let nothing come between us again.

CM Books, LLC

CM Books, LLC

# Chapter Fourteen

## Katie

With my arms wrapped around Linc's middle, we pulled into the parking lot to the Haven MC after we talked with the firemen and then the police on what took place in my front yard. Linc, Hawk, and even the Matherson brothers had helped smooth everything over. I was still having a problem believing that my home was now encased with yellow crime scene tape and do not enter warnings posted around about the structure not being sound.

My insurance company was contacted and the owner of the condo, too. The inside of the condo was left with mostly smoke and water damage. The quick response from the fire department had kept major damage from the fire down to the front rooms. The upstairs we were told received only smoke damage, but the stairs that led to the upper floor had been on fire and were too unstable to go up, which meant I wasn't able to retrieve any of my belongs. I didn't know what I would have done if I had been there by myself when all that took place. I had no plans to run that scenario over in my mind. Instead, I placed my focus on the man in front of me who was currently parking the bike.

He barreled his way back into my life, and even though I hated the fact he left me, I could never bring myself to hate him. So it made no sense to waste more time fighting with him over past mistakes when in the end, it was his cockiness and the sweetness he shared only with me, the tough exterior, and his ability to make every moment with him cherishable. All the things that had drawn me to him in the first place even at the young age of six.

Linc may have said I was his when he was eight years old, but he hadn't realized the moment I pushed him into the pool that day, he'd become mine. There's not a memory from growing up that he was not part of—good or bad.

The bike shut off and Linc patted my arms that were wrapped tight around his waist.

"You can let go now, babe. You did good. I'll make a biker chick out of you before this is over," he said as I let go of him and dismounted the bike. He held onto me until my legs steadied, then he dismounted.

We stood by the bike while the others pulled in. Charlie took the spot beside us and kicked the stand down, then threw her leg over the bike with a skill I didn't think I would ever master no matter how used to being on a bike I became.

"I still don't get why I have to come here and stay when the firemen said they didn't find any reason I couldn't stay at my place. The fire hadn't even made it to your garage,

CM Books, LLC

not even the smell of smoke lingered. Plus, I could just as easily stay in a hotel," Charlie started in no sooner than she took her helmet off and sat it on the seat of her bike.

"They didn't say you could stay there because nothing was wrong with your place. They said they didn't *see* anything wrong, but the place needed to be inspected to make sure before you could go in," I told her and smiled.

"Girl, that is just a technicality. Can you not let me gripe for two minutes? I mean," she looked around the lot at the few men who were outside when we pulled up and then back at me, "it's not like this is a hardship. Just, damn."

I chuckled, and Linc shook his head. As soon as Hawk and the Matherson brothers walked up, we headed for the door to the clubhouse. Outside I could faintly hear the music, when the door was opened, well, I was left with no doubt that a party was taking place.

Linc led me with his hand at the small of my back, and we were followed by Charlie, then Hawk and the Mathersons: Josh, Jake, Mitchell, and Travis. The main room to the clubhouse was large and full. Charlie stepped beside me and slid her arm through mine.

"I've been missing out my entire life. If all motorcycle clubs are filled with hot ass men, someone has been keeping a big fucking secret. Damn, this is like walking through the chocolate aisle in the grocery store—everything looks good, and you find yourself unable to make a choice. I could totally deal with that part, 'cause I so believe in samples." I looked around as we made our way through, and so did Charlie. However, I think it was for different reasons.

157

A woman in a tight-fitting tank that cut across the bottom of her breasts while the top part of it left her breasts spilling out, and a short skirt that ended right at her butt cheeks, was heading right for us. She stopped right in front of Linc, and I watched him stiffen when the woman ran her hand over his chest. He looked at me, and I lifted my brow.

"Moose, I haven't seen you since you left me in bed the other day," the woman said with the whiniest voice I had ever heard. And when she spoke, she glanced over at me and then back at Linc. I knew the statement she was trying to make for my benefit.

Charlie squeezed my arm and leaned in. "Don't you just hate catty bitches?" I assumed Charlie's voice was supposed to be a whisper, but she said it loud enough for the others around us to hear, especially the woman who cut her eyes over to Charlie.

"Ginger, don't start crap or I'll have you escorted out and you'll be told not to return," Linc said to the woman and removed her hand from his chest.

"I wasn't starting anything, hon. Just stating facts." Ginger cut her eyes to Charlie and me, and I knew the woman wasn't finished. "The bottled redhead, now she wants to start something."

Charlie snorted. "Please, my hair is natural. And really, of all people, you should be able to tell the difference. I mean between your own dyed hair to your fake tits and don't even get me started on the rest—your lips, around your eyes, and your thighs have all seen more needles than an acupuncturist uses on their clients."

Linc and Hawk burst out laughing, and the Mathersons at least tried to control themselves by covering their laughter with fake coughs. When the woman sneered at Charlie, I knew the situation needed to be put to rest before it got totally out of hand.

Linc was a gorgeous man, I wasn't delusional that he hadn't slept with any women while we weren't together. But I could make it known that he wouldn't be sleeping with anyone but me from now on, which I'm sure if I took of this one, any others would no doubt be told, and I wouldn't have to continue to go through this on a regular basis.

"Ginger, was it? I get that you've slept with Linc, I mean, Moose. Hell, for all I know you could have been a regular in his bed...but," Linc looked down at me like I had lost my mind. I wanted to laugh at his expression, but it held together and continued, "he no longer will be available for you, or any of the other women he's been with. He is mine, and I don't share. Also, I don't want to hear about you or the other's time with him, it's rude and makes you come across as a skank. I'm sure that's not what you want to be considered as. So please share with the others what I am about to tell you—I'm a doctor, and I know every point on the body that can be used to bring maximum pain without leaving any evidence if it is touched the right way, soo..." I didn't get to finish before Ginger huffed and stomped away. The men around me laughed and when I looked up at Linc, he was smiling.

"Damn, sweetheart, you got a mean streak."

I smiled back at him. "Don't forget it. But, Linc?"

"Yeah, Katie."

"She is the prime example of why condoms are necessary."

The laughter grew around us and then stopped just as quickly when an older man stepped in front of Linc with several men who had to be close to Linc and Hawk's age. His eyes settled on me as he spoke to Linc.

"Moose, she is going to make a fine addition to Haven. You've chosen well in an ol' lady." The man smacked Linc on the shoulder.

"Thanks, Prez. This is Katie." Linc then turned to me, "Katie, this is Haven's president, Wild Bill."

"Nice to meet you, sir." I stuck my hand out, and he looked down at it before taking it and pulling me into a hug.

"Welcome to Haven. Call me Prez or Wild Bill, darlin'. I'll answer to either." He released me and stepped back and from the looks on the men's faces, that was not the way he regularly greeted people. "And who are you?" Wild Bill asked as his eyes moved from me to Charlie.

"Charlie Rhoades. Thanks for allowing me to come here." Charlie smiled at him.

"Anytime. Beautiful women brighten this place up with all these ugly mugs running around here."

I had a feeling that Wild Bill was a charmer under his leathers. And I was seeing a whole new side of my new friend as she giggled at his words. I looked over my shoulder when I heard Hawk mumble.

"Oh, for fuck's sake." And evidently, Wild Bill didn't suffer from any hearing issues either.

160

"What is your problem, Hawk?" Wild Bill asked.

"Nothing, Prez. I don't know how much time she's going to be able to spend here since she's going to work for this bunch." He used his thumb to point over his shoulders at the Mathersons. Wild Bill followed the direction of Hawk's hand, and a grin split his face.

"Finally come to join Haven?"

"Nah, Wild Bill. I don't think the club's ready for us. But I do have to say I appreciate the atmosphere around here," Travis said. I got the impression he was the oldest of the brothers. However, the four looked close in age, and from what I'd seen so far, they would fit in with the men of Haven easily. The brothers were tall, close in height with Linc's six foot five, their hair was coal black, and they even shared the same smoky gray eye color. Not to mention the way their clothes fit their bodies, I was sure they were just as tone underneath, too.

"You did a solid today for Haven showing up when you did. You come around anytime you want for the atmosphere. You boys will always be welcome," Wild Bill said and moved around us to shake each of their hands. "Now, enjoy the party while I borrow these men for a few." The Mathersons nodded and headed for the bar that sat in the corner. Charlie turned to follow them, and Hawk stopped her.

"You need to go with Katie to the kitchen where the other ol' ladies are. You got no business out here with the men." Charlie tilted her head back to look up at Hawk.

Linc's muttered, "Oh hell," had me looking up at him. When he looked at me, he grinned. I'd have to remember to ask him later what the hell that meant, though I was pretty sure it had to do with the interest I saw not only in Charlie by Hawk, but Charlie's interest in him.

When I looked at Charlie, her eyes were shooting fire, and I had to admit I actually wondered if Haven had a first aid kit or fire extinguisher because Hawk might be in need of one.

"I'm not an ol' lady as you put it, so I guess that means I don't have to go in the kitchen. If you're worried one of the men in this room is going to jump me, well don't. You should be more worried that I'll jump them! I'm going to have a beer, and then if I feel like it, I might go to the kitchen. So, unless you have a rule that I can't have a beer at the bar with my bosses then... Fuck. Off." Charlie moved around him and walked to the bar. Hawk's eyes followed her, and when he turned back, the others started me chuckled, including Wild Bill. If I had to guess, Hawk wasn't used to women defying him.

"What? She doesn't need to be out here. She's not a hang-around nor is she part of this club." Hawk frowned at the others.

"Geez if this shit isn't going to be fun to watch," one of the men said that had walked up with Wild Bill.

"Fuck off, Keg. You know how the guys get after they've had too much to drink. They want to fuck, and they don't care who with." Hawk crossed his arms over his chest.

"I think it is more that you're afraid you will be in the meeting and that damn hot ass of hers will be riding one of our brothers."

Linc moved and stepped in between the two when Hawk stepped toward Keg. I was ready to reach for Linc because I didn't want him to get caught in a fight. Hawk's chuckle had me dropping my hand. I wasn't sure I'd ever understand these men.

"Oh, wait, that's right. Doesn't your advice on claiming a woman go something like—just kiss the shit out of her?" The biker Hawk called Keg asked, then laughed. The only thing I could do was look between the two men. I never felt more out of my element.

"Enough, both of you. I like to get to Church if you ladies are done bickering. Linc, take Katie to the kitchen and introduce her to Tink and Macy. They're the only two ol' ladies here. Meet us in my office when you're done."

"Sure thing, Prez. Come on, Katie." Linc put his arm around my shoulder and led me away. We went down a hall and when we reached the end, it opened into a huge kitchen that was set up for quite a few people to eat in at once. The two women sitting at the table looked up and at us when we entered.

"Who you got, Moose?" one of the women asked as they both stood.

"Tink, Macy, this is Katie, my ol' lady." Both women's eyebrows went up, and then the biggest smiles spread across their faces.

"We've often wondered which one of you was going to go down first. And it turned out to be our big Sergeant of Arms who's taken the fall first," Macy said and smiled up at Linc. I'd just learned about Moose's position earlier that day when I asked about the vest he wore and what everything on it meant. As I looked at the two women, they wore similar vests with their names on them.

"I have, Macy. Katie is going to hang in here with you women while I'm in Church." Linc turned to me. "I'll come to get you as soon as I'm done, sweetheart." He wrapped me in his arms and leaned down and kissed me. The kiss had my knees going weak, and when he released me, I was breathless and panting. "Stay in here, okay?" I nodded, which was all I could do. He chuckled and was gone before I retained the ability to speak.

"Come on, hon. Have a seat and I'll get you something to drink." Tink led me over to the table and I sat with Macy. Tink fixed me a glass of iced tea and joined us.

"Seeing you young ones together reminds me of my first days with Fire. That man made my toes curl," Macy said dreamily.

"Oh hell, Macy, you said that last week when you were over at the house," Tink said.

"Yeah, that is what is great. He might have a little snow on the roof, but it hasn't affected the fire below." Macy laughed at her own joke, and I smiled at both women.

"Macy and I are ol' ladies to brothers. Not just club brothers, blood brothers. Her old man is Fire and mine is Smoke."

"Is there a story behind Fire and Smoke names, too?" I asked, and both women laughed. "What?"

"We'll tell you the story behind our old men's names if you tell us why yours is called Moose." I laughed, and they both smiled.

"I'm thinking with the smile she's wearing and the kiss we just witnessed, she got a good one to tell," Macy said, and I laughed harder. The women were great.

"Well, I thought it was in reference to you know…" I chuckled when both women's eyes went wide.

Tink slapped the table. "I always wondered if that was the case."

"Umm… not that it couldn't be, but they said it was because of his temper and bullheadedness."

Macy and Tink laughed harder. Macy was the first to pull herself together. "You're so easy. We knew the reason behind his road name. We were just teasing you."

I grinned and relaxed as we talked and laughed. They explained my role as Moose's ol' lady, and why the back of their vest said, 'Property Of' and their old man's name. I loved how they didn't make me feel stupid asking questions about something I knew little about, which I appreciated.

Charlie walked in not long after we sat down and joined right in. As I listened to the women talk, I couldn't even remember laughing so hard or having a better time.

165

CM Books, LLC

# Chapter Fifteen

## Moose

"She was the one that found the young girls for Stone and his boys to snatch and turn over to Kosnoff?" Wild Bill asked.

"Yeah. Sandy Mizer then got a cut and that was the bank account Pinch was looking into. The bitch was funneling the money through her hair salon's account. Feds picked her up this morning. She's talking, though, which is good 'cause the case against Stone is going to be so big that he and Jacks will never see the outside again. They will die in prison," I informed them of the last piece of info we were waiting for to clear Haven of the taint it cared for too long in my book.

"Here's the one that is going shock you. Mondo's Stone's kid."

"What?" Wild Bill said.

"Yeah, Sandy was living in the same trailer park as Stone back then. It was hot, and she had her door open

167

while she was watching TV. She fell asleep on the couch. And what woke her was Stone tearing her clothes off. He raped her, then told her he would come back and kill her if she told anyone. He then kept coming back. After she told him she was pregnant, he started to bring his friends with him and if she refused to do what they wanted, they held her down and forced her. They said since she was already knocked up what did it matter. And the sick part, the bastard made money off her being pregnant. It seems there are plenty of men out there who will pay money to fuck pregnant women. After Gavin was born, he came around at the beginning and still brought Jacks and Creeper with him, but they would only watch and jack off. Said they pass on touching her 'cause she felt looser from having the kid.

"Sandy told the Feds that is when the men got into young girls. Anyway, Stone kept coming around until Carly's mom showed up. Sandy said then he paid her money to keep her quiet about Gavin. Sandy put herself through beauty school and opened her shop with the cash. She was going to move out of the trailer park, but Stone wouldn't let her. By then he was already working for Kosnoff, money was good, but when he got into the trafficking part he needed young girls, that is where Sandy's shop came in. She picked girls who would come in to have their hair done. The woman is sick. Feds are going to have a mental evaluation done on her."

"They don't need to pay for an investigation, I can tell them the bitch is mental," Keg said. "Also, it answers a lot with Gavin."

CM Books, LLC

"Yeah, Gavin joined Haven to get back at Stone, when Stone took off, he gave him just enough info to keep Stone happy, all the while Gavin was taking his spot with Kosnoff. Now if we could find Mondo and Slick, we could have the whole group locked up," I said, and the others agreed with a variety of curse words thrown in for good measure.

Gavin and Slick were on the run. Wild Bill, Crank, Pinch, Tram, and Keg had gone to the apartment the two shared, and the only thing in it was furniture, their personal belongings gone. They shouldn't be too hard to locate because they would have to have their bikes stashed somewhere, those they wouldn't leave behind, which meant they would dump the SUV or pulling a trailer with the bikes in sight. My brothers tossed the place and came up with nothing that would link the pair to Kosnoff, but I knew they had to be the new guys that moved in to take over and that is why Kosnoff cut Stone and his boys out.

"What the fuck is wrong with people? Selling young girls off. Why would you even want a young girl?" Crank grumbled.

"Because greed is a powerful thing. The girls aren't their kids, so it doesn't matter to them, only the money," Wild Bill said and shook his head. "But it takes a perverted sick bastard to buy one of those girls for personal use. The others are like Kosnoff, they are in it for the money. They put the girls in stables, and by the time the girls are used up, they've made a fortune off them. They keep a rotation of fresh meat coming in and it keeps their buyers happy, and

CM Books, LLC

them rolling in the green. Kosnoff just happens to like playing in his stables."

"Sick," Keg said disgustedly, and I had to agree.

I wasn't the only one when Tram smacked Keg's back and said, "Agreed, brother."

"Damn, I'm going to get my ass chewed out by Madison when they seize that account and she finds out what is going on. I might need to take a vacation," Pinch said, and we laughed. Madison was his younger sister that he raised after their parents were killed in a boating accident. Pinch had just turned nineteen and still fresh in the military. The military had been a piece of cake compared to raising his fourteen-year-old sister. The Department of Social Services wanted to put her into foster care because of his age and the fact that he could be deployed and where would that leave Madison, but he fought for her, and he won. He stayed in the military until his enlistment was up and bailed, joining Haven MC shortly after.

"So, Katie's part? Why was she targeted by them today?" Wild Bill asked.

"Still not positive it was Mondo and Slick. So until we catch them, not sure why Katie is being targeted," I said, and everyone's eyes turned toward me. "What?"

"Brother, we know you. What does your mind and gut tell you?" Keg asked.

Keg was right, I had my suspicions and my gut was aching. I looked around the table, then let my brothers in on my thoughts, "Well, Kosnoff was infatuated with Katie. He had been for a while. At least back to her graduation from medical school. He was using traditional methods to win her attention. However, I think if she continued to ignore him like she was, she would have become one of the snatched. He would have probably taken her to Russia and hidden her away. With Kosnoff hiding out, the others blamed Katie for their income loss. Who knows, they may have planned to snatch her today if not for the Mathersons showing up. They had clear shots at Hawk and me. Hell, they could have killed us easily since neither one of us were carrying. Then they could have grabbed Katie and Charlie. Like I said before. Until we find them, we won't know what they had planned for Katie. That is if it was them. If it wasn't Mondo and Slick, then we have some unidentified players we need to locate," I finished.

"Bet you won't forget your guns again," Crank said.

"Fuck, I left mine on the counter at the house when Taylor stopped by to get Moose's bike. I decided to just pull out with them and never went back in the damn house," Hawk said with disgust.

"What about you, Moose? Where was yours? You're always carrying," Keg asked.

"In my saddlebags. I couldn't get to it while I was covering Katie." I expected some flak for that, but none of them said a thing.

"Shit, what we all should have done was make a run for Charlie's garage. She had it opened just as the hit happened. When we closed it up after the fire was out, I looked in there. The woman has two gun cabinets up against the back wall. If we had made it there, those bastards

171

wouldn't have had a chance to leave except maybe in body bags," Hawk said, and we chuckled. Hawk took everything seriously and as far as with what happened, no doubt he looked at it as a failure on our part for not being prepared. I did. And I would damn sure not make that mistake again.

"Okay, so we have to wait for Gavin and Slick to turn up or do we search for them?" Wild Bill asked and looked at each of us for input. It didn't escape me, or the others for that matter, that the Prez wasn't using Gavin's road name, Mondo. I was surprised he was stilling referring to Elliot's.

"They're the last of our troubles, I vote we hunt them down," Tram said.

"Me too," Crank replied.

"I'm in. I should have let Carly shoot that fucker that day. Never liked him," Keg said.

"We couldn't find Stone when he was running. What makes you think we'll have any better luck catching those two? They got a helluva good start on us," Hawk said.

"Because they have no money other than what's on them. Feds got their bank accounts frozen before they had time to empty them and they don't have Kosnoff to bankroll them like Stone did when he was running. Stone surfaced because he was out of money and pissed that he'd been replaced. He just didn't know his own son was pushing out."

"True. I'm in on catching the assholes," Hawk said.

"You know I want them, Prez. So count me in, too," I said.

CM Books, LLC

"Good, 'cause I figured we could also use the Matherson brothers to help out. Large territory covered if we get them on board," Wild Bill said and looked at all of us.

"That could work. With the job coming up, we need to locate them quickly. The extra help will make that possible." Everyone nodded in agreement.

"Alright, well, Church is officially over." Wild Bill banged the gavel. "Let's go have a beer and talk to Travis and his brothers. Make sure they aren't on any jobs."

"Okay, I'll meet you at the bar after I go check on Katie," I said as my phone rang. I pulled it out and looked at the screen to see that it was my dad.

"Hey, pops." My expression must have told the others something was wrong because instead of heading out the door, they stopped to listen.

"Yeah! No shit. Okay. Okay. I'll let her know. Sure, sounds good. Thanks, pops." I disconnected the call and took a deep breath.

"What's going on?" Wild Bill asked.

"The Feds have Gavin and Slick. We were right with them needing money. They called Paul, Katie's dad, an acted as an agent for the Feds and told him they forgot to grab a file that they needed from his office. He told them he'd meet them at the firm. The silent alarm went off, which sent the cops there. And they caught the assholes trying to get into the safe in my dad's office. Paul gave them the combination when they put a knife to his throat, he didn't know my dad had it changed when all the shit went down with him."

"How did your dad get ahold of this information?" Wild Bill asked.

"There were cameras installed a few years ago that he can activate at his house if the alarm system to the firm goes off. That way, he would know what was going on and two, it would help let the cops know if there was actually someone in the place and how many."

"Well, that system was worth however much money he spent on it," Prez said.

"No shit. He bitches about it all the time. Complains about the monthly fees and the maintenance contract he purchased when he had it installed. I'll take bets he doesn't complain anymore," I said.

"Now that we don't have to get a hunting party together. How about we just have a beer? I think we all fucking deserve it," Prez said and smiled at each of us. "I want to thank each one of you for sticking by me. It's been a long ass road, but it's almost over. Now we can turn our focus on Haven's future."

"Anything for you, Prez," Hawk said, and we all agreed.

"Okay, let's go get that beer before someone starts hugging." Crank shoved Keg, and we chuckled.

"I'm going to go check on Katie and tell her what happened. She's going to want to know her dad is alright." I started out the door, and the others followed. "Hey, where is Roach? I didn't see him when we came in. He's always around," I asked.

CM Books, LLC

"He called early said he was staying home, wasn't feeling too well," Prez answered.

"Damn, he doesn't need to go to the doctor, does he?" I asked because Roach was one of Haven's older members. The man was never sick.

"I asked him and he said no that he just needed to rest. Said it was nothing but his arthritis acting up. I was concerned at first since nothing keeps the man down until he went on a ten-minute rant about getting old and cutting the next person he heard say how great the golden years were," Wild Bill said as we hit the main room.

Chuckling, I turned toward the kitchen and out of the corner of my eye, I saw Hawk look around the room before he turned and followed me.

When we walked in, Macy and Tink were at the stove pulling cookies out of the oven. I looked around, but there was no Katie or Charlie in sight. "Where is Katie?"

"Oh, she and Charlie needed to pee," Tink said as she put the pan down on the counter.

"Did you point in the direction of the one off the main room?" I asked.

"No. The one at the bottom of the stairs is closer." Macy pointed to the door that led to the common room and where Shock's and Freak's rooms were.

Shit, my gut squeezed. "Goddammit, Shock and Freak have never met Katie, Macy. You know how those two get when there's a party going on up here." I headed toward the door with Hawk on my heels.

CM Books, LLC

"Oh shit, we are so sorry, Moose. I didn't think of that," Tink said and came around the counter as if to follow. Hawk told the women to stay upstairs as we both reached the door at the same time.

I threw the door open and trotted down the stairs. When I reached the bottom the bathroom door stood open, showing there was no one inside.

I turned the corner with Hawk right behind me just as laughter was heard. What we saw made both of us stop in our tracks.

Hawk leaned in and whispered, "What the hell?"

Katie and Charlie sat on one of the couches, their legs pulled and bent under them, and each had a beer in their hands. In the two chairs across from them sat Shock and Freak. They too had beers in hand.

Shock noticed us first and looked in our direction. "Hey, brothers. How ya doing?"

"Hey, Linc, is Church over?" Katie said and smiled brightly at me.

"Didn't I tell you to stay with the women?" I asked her, probably a little more sternly than I should have since her smile turned into a frown.

"Oh, leave the girl alone. She and Charlie have been keeping two old men company. And, Moose, you did well, brother. I like her," Freak said and tipped his beer toward me.

"Did we walk into the fucking Twilight Zone or what?" Hawk mumbled behind me, and I looked over my shoulder at him. "What? You are just as surprised as I am."

176

He was right, but I wasn't going to tell him that. Shock and Freak didn't like people in their space. Well, the exception being the brothers in Haven that they liked, which was few.

"Hawk, you'd do well to snatch up Charlie. The girl has got it going on. Did you know she's a bounty hunter? If she caught you jumping bail, why would anyone care? Hell, though I might put up a little resistance at first to get her to wrestle me down," Shock, singing Charlie's praises chuckled.

"Yeah, Hawk," I said over my shoulder.

"Shut up, asshole," Hawk said and hit my shoulder as he passed by me.

"Linc, did you know Steven and Frankie were POWs?" Katie said as I walked over to where she was sitting.

"Umm...yeah." I looked at Hawk and he shrugged.

I was going to have to find out exactly what went on when I took Katie home. Shock and Freak never talked about their POW time. And they sure as hell didn't go around sharing their real names with people.

"They've been telling Charlie and me tales about their experiences in the military," Katie said, and all I could think was how fucking long had the women been in the basement. I hadn't realized I'd said it out loud until Katie answered.

"Oh, I don't know. Charlie, how long have we been down here?" she turned to her friend who shrugged.

"Beats me. We came down to the bathroom and when we came out that's when you noticed the snake," Charlie said.

"That's right. Then we played with Jasmine and Freak showed us his other snake." Charlie laughed, and Katie shook her head. "Not *that* snake, you ass."

Hawk turned and looked at me and cocked his brow. Maybe VP was right, and we did step into an episode of the Twilight Zone. "Katie? Babe? Focus. You saw Jasmine and played with her?" Christ, I wouldn't even touch the snake.

"Sure, she is a sweetheart."

"Moose, she wasn't scared at all. Neither was Charlie." Freak went on to explain how Katie was great with the snake. I waited for him to finish so I could tell Katie about her dad.

When Freak stopped for a drink, I took the opening, "Katie, your dad is fine, but there was an incident at the firm."

"What happened?" she asked and her expression went from happy to worried. We talked about everything while we'd been locked away in her place. I knew she struggled with everything her dad had done and if she hadn't needed to know, I would have kept the information to myself to give her a few minutes of fun and relaxation.

She listened as I told her about Gavin and Slick and what they had done.

"Well the whole family should be in jail," Katie said and leaned back against the couch.

"Under the damn thing is where they should put them. What a bunch of losers," Charlie added.

CM Books, LLC

"You aren't going to get any argument from me. We are going to have a celebratory beer for this shit. You ladies are more than welcome to come up and join us," I said.

"Sure. Come on, Steven and Frankie," Katie said. I would have to tell Katie once we got upstairs that Shock and Freak didn't mean anything by telling her no. They just didn't do well with a large crowd and loud music.

Instead, I was sure my mouth dropped when Shock spoke, "Right behind, honey."

"Wouldn't miss it, sweetie," Freak said and rose out of the chair.

"Told you, brother. Twilight Zone," Hawk leaned in and whispered.

"Knock it off. These two are sweethearts," Charlie said as she looked over her shoulder and frowned at Hawk.

I helped Katie up and pulled her close, then bent and kissed the top of her head. We started toward the stairs as the others followed. A crashing sound had us stopping and turning around.

"What the fuck!" Hawk yelled as we watched Alexi Viktor Kosnoff walk through the door that led from the back entrance.

"Who the fuck are you?" Shock asked.

Katie started to tremble, and I pulled her tighter to me. "Why the fuck are you here, Kosnoff?" I asked as he pointed the gun in his hands right at us.

"I came for Kathryn. I leaving the country, and I will need her to come with me."

"Are you fucking crazy?" Charlie said, drawing Kosnoff's attention to her.

"Well, well. You can come along, too. Your hair is absolutely beautiful, and I'm positive the bidding for you will bring top dollar."

Hawk looked at me while Kosnoff's focused on Charlie. We knew he couldn't shoot everyone at once, but it would be better if we could take him down without anyone taking a bullet. The man had evidently lost his mind if he thought he would walk out of Haven's clubhouse.

Besides, he didn't have an automatic, he was pointing a six-shot pistol. The man was definitely short a few brain cells to break into any MC's clubhouse when the majority of bikers carried much bigger hardware. He might have well brought a knife to a gun fight. His odds might have been better.

"Yeah, that's going to fucking happen. Not!" Charlie said. The woman was good, if she kept him focused on her, Hawk and I could move in on him.

"You will need some work. The men in Russia who will pay for such beauty will not put up with so much disrespect. You will learn, though. And if I can't break you, I'll just turn you over to my men for usage. They will fuck the disrespect out of you," Kosnoff said and the whole time Hawk and I stepped closer and closer.

"Come here, Kathryn, you and your friend. My car is down the block. We will have a nice walk." Hawk and I stopped where we were when Kosnoff turned in our direction to speak to Katie.

CM Books, LLC

A shot was fire and before I realized what took place, I watched the gun drop out of Kosnoff's hand. He grabbed his wounded arm with his other to stifle the flow of blood seeping from the bullet hole.

Hawk moved and picked up the gun while I grabbed Kosnoff and took him to the floor. When I had the man contained, I glanced around and found who had shot Kosnoff. Freak sat in the chair holding a gun still pointed in Kosnoff's direction.

"And people say Shock and I are crazy. Sorry if I stepped in at the wrong time, but the man was giving me a headache with his rambling."

Before anyone could reply, the sound of feet running down the stairs had everyone turning in that direction to watch. Wild Bill and half the club as they barreled into the common room, guns were drawn as they stopped and took in the scene.

"You're gonna want to call your Fed buddies, Prez. They're going to need to make another pickup," Shock said as he walked to Katie and put his arm around her, whispering to her so low I couldn't hear what he was saying to her and doubted if anyone else could.

Latch walked over and took my place with Kosnoff. I walked to Katie and Shock let her go and moved toward Freak. I opened my arms, and she fell into them. I hugged her tight, closed my eyes for a second, and enjoyed the feeling of having her close.

"You going to be okay, babe?" I asked while I held her tight.

"Yeah, I think so. It's over, huh?" She asked as she leaned her head back to look at me.

"Should be."

"I wonder what this means for my dad," she said and laid her head against my chest.

It took me a minute to answer her. The way it went down with Kosnoff could have easily gone another way. Instead of him down with a bullet hole, Katie could have been. I took a deep breath and released it slowly because she was safe in my arms, and I wouldn't run through 'what ifs.'

"The Feds will honor the deal with him. The attorney my dad hired for him will make sure of it, sweetheart, but everyone is safe, and that's what counts. The rest we can deal with." I squeezed her again just because I could.

"Sorry to interrupt, but the Feds are on their way. Why don't you take Katie home, Moose? The Feds can talk with you and her later. I think Katie has had enough excitement for today." Prez patted Katie's back as he walked by.

"Charlie, you want to come with us? You're welcome to stay at my place." Charlie had gone over and stood by the Mitchell Matherson who had been one of the men to come down with Wild Bill.

"Thanks, but while I was upstairs, the landlord called me. They got a building inspector to come out and check my place. It is good to go. I can go back home."

"That's great news. Call if you need anything, okay?" Katie said, and Charlie walked over. I let loose of Katie and the two women hugged.

As we got ready to head up the stairs, Freak walked up, followed by Shock. I could feel every member's eyes, who was in the common room, on us.

"Are you going to be okay, sweetie?" Freak asked Katie, and she turned and hugged him.

"Thank you, Frankie. And yes, I'm going to be fine." Katie stepped back from Freak and then turned and hugged Shock.

"Thank you, too, Steven. I had a wonderful time talking to you both. We will have to do it again."

"You bet, anytime, darlin'. Now let your man take you home and put you to bed." Katie nodded and grabbed hold of my arm.

As we started up the stairs, I asked, "Should I be worried?"

Katie laughed, and it was the best thing I'd ever heard.

CM Books, LLC

# Chapter Sixteen

## Katie

The sun was shining in the room when I opened my eyes and looked around. The room was huge and decorated in shades of blue and gray. It had been dark when we pulled up to the house last night, and all I could tell in the dark was that it was a huge log house. We parked in the garage and went through the door that led into the kitchen and the only thing in that room I noticed was the appliances shining in the soft glow of the stove light that had been left on. It had been the extent of my viewing because, with everything that had taken place, I was exhausted.

Linc walked me through the house, and we entered the master suite, which was on the first floor. I remembered he told me the upstairs held three other bedrooms.

I felt him behind me, his breaths even and deep telling me that he still slept. A lot had happened in less than a week, but as I laid curled into him, I wouldn't have changed a thing. His cock twitched behind me, and I pushed back

185

against it and stifled the moan that wanted to escape. The arm draped over me moved, and the hand splayed across my breasts. When the hand started to caress them, the nipples turned to hardened peaks and I felt myself growing wet. My hand moved to the waist of my panties and I wiggled until I had them down to my ankles and then I kicked them off. I pressed my butt back against Linc, and his cock twitched again, its hard length pressed into the crack of my butt. I did it once more, and his hand moved to squeeze my breast, and then he tweaked the nipple. I couldn't hold back the moan as I had before.

"You trying to wake him, babe?" Linc said sleepily and rocked his hips into mine 'causing his erection to slide up and down the crack.

"Yes," was the only thing I could force out, the sensation of him pinching and tweaking my nipples along with his velvet covered steel sliding up and down the crack of my butt was leaving me damn near speechless.

"Well, I think you succeeded."

His hand left my breasts to slide down, and he lifted my leg, pulled it back and sat it on his hip, opening me wide. This time when he rocked his hips, he slipped between my thighs and came in contact with my now soaked center. Linc kept rocking, and the friction of him sliding through my folds had me growing wetter. His hand moved off my leg, and he positioned it on my mound as his middle finger rested on my clit. He began to circle the bud until it hardened and felt like it had its own pulse. Linc kept the slow

CM Books, LLC

and steady pace, and with every pass he made with the finger, my core spasmed. I needed him inside me.

"Please."

"My woman woke horny this morning. Does she need me to take care of her?"

"Yes, so could you please stop torturing me." I could feel the wetness on my inner thigh.

Linc rolled onto his back and pulled me with him. "I'm still tired. You need to do a little of the work."

I didn't know how, but I ended up facing him and straddling his hips. His erection pressed into my center and a shiver ran through me.

"You gonna ride me, babe?"

I leaned up and positioned myself to take him inside me. Easing down until the feeling of being stuffed full would have been an understatement. Linc groaned as I shifted to adjust to his size and get more comfortable.

"You're going to have to move, babe, you're killing me," Linc gritted out. I moved my arms behind me and rested my hands on thighs to balance me as I used my legs to help me raise and lower on him. I started out slow, my wetness allowing him to slide in and out of me with ease.

The tightness started in my belly and worked its way down to my core, causing my inner walls to spasm around him on every down stroke. Linc's hands held my hips and helped steady me.

I knew the second he'd had enough of the slow pace I set. When in a fluid motion, he rose and shifted us until I was my knees with my head and shoulders pushed into the bed. One arm held his weight off me while the other rubbed up and down my back as he moved in and out of me.

"I'm awake now."

"I'm close," I moaned out, and he picked up the pace. His cock kissing my cervix with each inward stroke. I felt the hand move down my back until it rested on my rear and his thumb pressed through the crack to circle my back hole. The sensation had me pushing back against the pressure. "Linc, please."

"I'll always take care of your needs, sweetheart," he said, and pushed his thumb through the ring of muscle into my back hole, then he pumped it in and out in sync with his thrusts. He pulled his thumb out, and I felt the loss only to be full again as he replaced it with one of his large fingers, enabling him to go deeper. He added another finger, and I was sure I was going to go over the edge. "Wait and go with me, babe."

I didn't know if I could stop the orgasm that was building as he began to scissor his fingers, twisting them with downward strokes, stretching me. The bite of pain I felt was quickly gone with a powerful need to come.

"I need to come, Linc!"

"A little longer, hold it a little longer." His own voice showed signs of a struggle.

I felt the loss as he placed his weight on his knees, moving the hand from the bed to hold onto my hip. My legs trembled and I gritted my teeth as I tried to hold out for him. When he stopped and his hand left my hip, then the bed shifted behind me, I wanted to scream. I was so close.

CM Books, LLC

The bed shifted again, and he pulled out. I was ready to scream at him when I heard the buzzing sound.

"Thought we could play." He flipped me onto my back, draped my legs over his thighs, opening me wide. He moved the vibrator through my juices, then pushed it inside me. My scream filled the room when I couldn't keep the orgasm from taking over. My body still shook as I felt pressure on my back hole and then a bite of pain as he pushed his cock past the ring and onward at an excruciatingly slow pace until he was fully seated in my ass. The vibrator pushed inside as he pulled back and then reversed. My own hips thrust to meet his. "That's it, babe, take me. You're so tight, and you feel so good."

He continued to fuck me, and yes, it was pure fucking, and I loved it. The things he was doing to me were... No words could explain the feelings I was experiencing.

I felt the beginning of another orgasm building, and my body began to shake as it pushed through.

"Go with me, Katie!" Linc yelled, pushed himself deep into my back hole and the vibrator deep inside my pussy. That was all it took, and we went over together. I felt the warmth from his cum as the tremors from the aftermath of the most explosive orgasm racked my body.

A few minutes later after we were able to move, I regained the ability to speak, "Damn, I'm going to have to wake you more often."

Linc chuckled, then got out of the bed and entered the bathroom. As I waited for him to return, I closed my eyes.

The warm cloth touching the oversensitive skin on my lower body brought out a moan.

After he finished tenderly cleaning me, he took the cloth back to the bathroom, then climb back into the bed.

"You can wake me anytime," he said and kissed my forehead before laying his head beside mine.

I rolled to face him and braced my head on my hand and looked down at him as he laid with his eyes closed. "Linc, what I saw of your house last night, I loved. I would love to see the rest of it today and the grounds around. It's a log home, right?"

He was quiet, and I thought he had fallen back to sleep until he took a deep breath and opened his eyes.

When he only watched me, I asked, "What?"

He smiled. "When I bought the property, an old farmhouse sat here. I had it torn down and had this place built."

"Well, it's beautiful."

"I built it for you."

I stared, and though I heard what he said, I didn't quite understand. "You built the house for me?"

"Yes. I had it built when you were in the last year of medical school. I wanted it ready when you graduated."

I felt the tears form in my eyes at the thought of him coming back to this house without me that day. He rolled to face me and placed my face in his hands, using his thumbs to wipe the tear away.

"I didn't tell you that to make you cry. The reason for this house being built is the same now as it was then. I built

190

the house because I want us to have a place to live in. A home to raise the children I want with you. A home, Katie, where I can spend every day loving you. A home we can grow old together in."

The tears came at a faster speed, and his hands held my face a little tighter. His eyes sparkled as they stared into mine.

"Marry me, Kathryn Stevens, so we can start that life together. Here."

Through my tears, I could envision everything he spoke about when I looked into his eyes. How could I not want the same?

"Yes. Yes!"

A few hours later, I finally got to see the rest of the house and the outdoors surrounding it. I couldn't believe the landscaping he'd done to the front and back yards. Every bush, flower, and tree were placed perfectly to not only compliment each other, but to flow as if every one of them had been in place naturally instead of planted for effect.

"It really is beautiful, Linc. You did an excellent job with it all," I said as we walked back toward the house.

"Thanks. Not going to say it was easy, but with my brothers' help, it didn't take as long as I thought it would to get it done. The hardest part has been keeping everything alive."

I chuckled. Then as we reached the pool, I stopped walking. "Does the pool get much use? You used to love swimming."

"Still do, it's great exercise. That's why I put the pool in. After I left, there wasn't a lot of time for swimming while in the military. Even now, I like to use it every day, but I'm lucky if I get to swim once a week."

"How about you? I recall you used to enjoy being in the water?"

I bent down and grazed my fingers over the top of the water, then stood back up and flick the droplets at Linc.

"I'll let you in on a secret. I only learned how to swim because I wanted to impress you. You were eight and paid little to no attention to me. I thought it was because I had to wear floaties while you were able to swim to the deep end. I begged for lessons. The day I pushed you in the pool, I had just finished my final lesson the day before and was looking forward to showing you my new skill. But before I could get in the pool, you walked up to me and said babies weren't allowed in the water without their floaties. So instead of me getting in the pool, I pushed you in."

"Ah, the day I fell in love," Linc said and threw his arm over my shoulder.

I bit my lip to keep from smiling as I looked up at Linc. "I think we need a renewal to our love."

Linc squeezed my shoulder. "Whenever you want, just tell me the day and we'll get hitched."

I smiled. "Who needs a wedding to renew our love." I shifted from under his arm.

"Then what the hell are you ta—" Linc's words were cut off as I shoved him off the side of the pool. I was

CM Books, LLC

giggling when he surfaced and shook the water from his hair and face.

"That was perfect," I said between giggles. "I enjoyed that just as much as I did when I was six. The only difference is I love you more today."

"Totally agree," Linc said as he made his way to the ladder. "Something else I loved about that day, too."

"What?"

Linc reached for the ladder and looked at me. "When I got out of the water and chased you, getting you wet once I caught you."

"Oh no, you better not. I had a bathing suit on then." My smile died at his words. Evidently, I hadn't thought my actions all the way through and the devilish grin I received confirmed my mistake.

"Trust me, no bathing suit necessary this time. I'm going to get you wet, it just isn't going to involve water." Linc said as he stepped out of the pool dripping, his t-shirt plastered to his chest and water seeping from his boots.

Shit.

"Linc, I'm on shift at the hospital in an hour," I said, gave him a once over, then turned and sprinted toward the back door to the house with his laughter and footsteps following me.

"Guess while I'm stripping out of these wet clothes you better call them and let them know you'll be a little late."

I slammed the door behind me, pulled my cell out of my pocket and jogged into the bedroom. I couldn't have stopped the smile from gracing my face if I had wanted to. Being in love felt great.

CM Books, LLC

# Epilogue

## Hawk

The hot shower felt good, but my couch felt better. It had been a long week clearing out Katie's condo so the owners could start the repairs. They'd had the stairs torn out and replaced them with a portable stairway. The furniture from the bedrooms were the only things that had to stay put until the new stairs were built. No way big ass men were going to make it down with heavy furniture on the temporary set. That would have been an accident in the making.

I was just glad that we finished up today. It had been hell working with Charlie every day. The more time I spent with her, the more I wanted her. It hadn't helped that every time she bent over to pick something up my dick hardened. Manual labor with a hard-on was not something I would recommend.

The Prez and Keg were headed out tomorrow to go to Ally's birthday party at Black Hawk MC and I would be left

CM Books, LLC

in charge until he came back. Then when they got back, we'd be leaving for the job in Boston. I was going to need that distance from a certain redhead.

I needed food, beer, and sleep. Or maybe I just needed to go to the clubhouse, grab one of the hang-arounds and fuck her until I forgot. Better yet, I just needed to get drunk. I got up and headed for the kitchen as the doorbell rang.

Fuckin' A. I turned back the way I came and opened the door expecting to see one of my brothers. Instead, it was the woman who had me jacking off like a teenage boy with one thought of her.

"What are you doing here?" I asked.

"Wow, you're welcoming. I brought food." She held out the pizza box. I took the box and stepped back so she could enter.

"And why are you bringing pizza to my house?"

"I didn't find out until today that you lived in the same neighborhood so... You eat, don't you?" That was a damn loaded question. She'd run and hide if I told her what I wanted to do to her.

"Yeah, I eat."

We walked in the living room, and I sat the pizza box on the coffee table. "Wanna beer to go with it?"

"Beer would be great."

I went to the kitchen, grabbed napkins, and went back in the living room and sat down.

I grabbed a slice of pizza and took a bite and Charlie turned to me. "Do you have a steady woman?"

CM Books, LLC

I turned and looked at her. With my mouth full, I shook my head.

"Good, I don't have to feel guilty when I let you fuck me."

CM Books, LLC

CM Books, LLC

# Acknowledgment

To the women who I have had the opportunity to meet through writing – this is for you. You make me work to do better with each book. Thank you.

*Carson*

CM Books, LLC

CM Books, LLC

# About the Author

Carson Mackenzie enjoys writing romance with a real feel inside the stories. She writes with the belief not every man is a jerk and not every woman needs saving.

Carson lives in the South with one of her sons, a Great Dane and two adopted shelter dogs that keep the household in line. Books have always been a part of her life. There is nothing better to her than curling up and relaxing with a good story and losing herself in someone else's world for a few hours.

Writing stories and growing as an author with each book is her goal. She wants to reach the level where a reader knows when they see her name, they can trust in the fact there will be a good story as they flip through the pages.

Carson's been her writing journey for a few years. As she's finally starting to settle in, her only regret is she hadn't started sooner.

**Stay up to date with what I'm working on:**

Webpage: www.carsonmackenzieauthor.com/
Goodreads:
www.goodreads.com/author/show/14764937.Carson_Mackenzie

CM Books, LLC

CM Books, LLC

# Books by Carson Mackenzie

## Black Hawk MC

Speed
Crusher
Devil
Ghost
Jag
Coast
Flirt

## Haven MC

Moose's Regret
Hawk's Bounty
Keg's Revelation

## Desert Phoenix MC

Desert Phoenix Rising

CM Books, LLC

## Standalones
Her Way or No Way
Two Paths One Destiny

CM Books, LLC

CM Books, LLC

www.ingramcontent.com/pod-product-compliance
Lightning Source LLC
Chambersburg PA
CBHW020906180626
46816CB00007BA/2265